SHOT INTO SILENCE . . .

"What? Who are you talking about? I don't know any Burnside."

"The telegrapher," Slocum said, his patience wearing thin. "I want the telegram."

"Slocum, look, it's this way. I—"

The shot caught Benton high in the chest, just below his throat. He slipped to the muddy shore of Mystic Lake, as dead as the fish washed up beside him . . .

DON'T MISS THESE
ALL-ACTION WESTERN SERIES
FROM THE BERKLEY PUBLISHING GROUP

THE GUNSMITH by J. R. Roberts

Clint Adams was a legend among lawmen, outlaws, and ladies. They called him . . . the Gunsmith.

LONGARM by Tabor Evans

The popular long-running series about U.S. Deputy Marshal Long—his life, his loves, his fight for justice.

LONE STAR by Wesley Ellis

The blazing adventures of Jessica Starbuck and the martial arts master, Ki. Over eight million copies in print.

SLOCUM by Jake Logan

Today's longest-running action Western. John Slocum rides a deadly trail of hot blood and cold steel.

JAKE LOGAN

PIKES PEAK SHOOT-OUT

BERKLEY BOOKS, NEW YORK

PIKES PEAK SHOOT-OUT

A Berkley Book / published by arrangement with the author

PRINTING HISTORY
Berkley edition / July 1994

ISBN: 0-425-14294-9

BERKLEY®
Berkley Books are published by The Berkley Publishing Group,
200 Madison Avenue, New York, New York 10016.
BERKLEY and the "B" design
are trademarks belonging to Berkley Publishing Corporation.

PRINTED IN THE UNITED STATES OF AMERICA

10 9 8 7 6 5 4 3 2 1

PIKES PEAK SHOOT-OUT

1

"Why split the loot four ways?" Phil Warren kicked back in the straight, rickety chair, hoisting his boots to the railing along Federal Street. Under the brim of Warren's Stetson, John Slocum saw cold chips of blue passing for eyes. Warren had ice running in his veins, and it showed.

"How you figurin' on increasin' your share?" came the slow Southern drawl from the far end of the boardwalk, where Slick Bob Durham whittled. Each thin pine shaving he carved slid off in a precise fashion, exactly the right length and width to form a perfect whistle. The razor-thin, tall, sinewy cowboy never looked over at Warren as he spoke, but a sense of coiled tension, like a stepped-on rattler, grew between them. Slocum knew he'd have to stop the two men before they got to shooting over nothing.

He had recruited both men for the bank robbery. He and Slick Bob went back a ways. They had worked the stagecoaches leaving Pueblo and Durango a year earlier, making a few dollars without having to fire more than a warning shot or two. The pickings hadn't been too lucrative, but there had been enough to live on for the winter. Slocum trusted Slick Bob enough to turn his back on him now and again, as long as he didn't make it a habit.

Phil Warren was a horse of another color. Slocum knew him by reputation. Warren had served two years of the five he had received, for cattle rustling, at Canon City Penitentiary, before getting out on parole from the governor. Slocum had never asked after the details of that parole. He reckoned Warren was riding along as a free man without too many lawmen on his trail. But the man was a stone killer, and Slocum didn't much trust him.

"We've been through the plan," Slocum said in his cold, level voice. "The three of us take the bank. And—"

"And that damned telegrapher sits on his lily white ass over at the Western Union office and gets a share for doing nothing," finished Warren. He crossed his arms over his broad chest, but Slocum saw the way Warren's hand came closer to the cross-draw holster he wore.

Slick Bob saw the motion, too, and shifted just a mite, turning so that his left side was toward Warren. In this position he could get to his own six-shooter, hanging at his right side—or more likely, Slocum decided, use the knife in his hand. He had seen Slick Bob kill a man with that folding pocket knife during a barroom brawl.

"That 'damned telegrapher,' as you've taken to calling him," Slocum said carefully, "made this robbery possible. We'd never have known that a hundred pounds of gold would be resting in the First Denver Bank's vault if Burnside hadn't taken the message."

"Too damn convenient, I say," Warren went on. Slocum didn't relax, but Slick Bob did. Just a mite. The tall, thin cowboy shot Slocum a glance and shook his head slightly, as if saying, "Go figure what's in Warren's head."

Slocum knew, and he didn't like it. These two and Matt Burnside were his partners, and partners didn't double-cross one another. The bank robbery had made coming to Denver worthwhile. He had drifted the better part of the winter, living off the money he and Slick Bob Durham had stolen down south, and the tedium was beginning to wear on him. He needed action, and finding any job worth doing was well nigh impossible. Denver was a boom town, but they didn't need the skills he had to offer.

"Don't go trustin' Burnside farther than you can see him," Warren went on, not letting the matter lie once he'd got his teeth into it. "He's never done anything like this before. You can tell by the way he gets all scared looking when he talks about it. The first time a lawman comes sniffin' around, he's gonna roll over and play 'scratch my belly.' He'll have us swinging from the gallows 'fore the sun sets, just so he can save his own worthless neck."

"He needs the money," Slocum said. He was no fool. Burnside had been nervous about approaching Slocum, but Slocum's reputation as a straight shooter had convinced the telegrapher of the wisdom of seeking help. He knew better than to try a robbery of this size by himself, and everything he'd said matched what Slocum would have expected from a man in a fifty-dollar-a-month telegrapher's job with Western Union.

Burnside stood to make ten years' salary in a single morning. Even if a reward were offered by the bank, there wouldn't be that kind of money in it. But would he cooperate if he got caught and the marshal told him he might not go to prison if he confessed and testified against his partners? Slocum didn't know how hard the core was in Matt Burnside, but he was willing to risk it. The young man looked to have what it took for a job this big.

"What time's it gettin' to be?" asked Slick Bob. He finished his whittling, glanced in Warren's direction, then folded the knife and tucked it into the pocket of his denims. Slocum knew the cowboy thought Warren to be defanged, for the moment, and so did he. The idle thought running through Slocum's head concerned Slick Bob's choice of clothing. No selfrespecting cowboy wore jeans. He rubbed his hands against his own canvas trousers and decided they could all wear morning coats with fancy pearl buttons, if they chose, after this robbery.

"You got the horses staked out for a quick ride?" he asked Warren.

"I know what I'm doing. The horses are waiting. We ride the first ones till they drop. The second bunch we ride almost as hard, and the third will bring us along this side of the Front Range and back to pick up the gold." Warren chuckled, as if finding this funny. "We can be in Utah before they get a posse mounted."

Slocum doubted that. The law in Denver was aggressive about protecting their town, and the bank wasn't likely to let them sashay off with a hundred pounds of gold. Still, they would lead any pursuit in circles and double back for their share of the gold. Burnside had been reticent about who the bullion belonged to and where it was headed, but he had been positive the First Denver Bank would be the repository for at least one night, and maybe two, until the bullion could be shipped back east.

"We won't be traveling that fast," Slocum pointed out. "We got to keep the posse occupied while Burnside gets off with the wagon. There's no way we could hope to escape carrying that much with us on horseback."

"I don't agree. We ought to divvy it up right away. At the first horse switch-off," Phil Warren declared. "Twenty-five pounds of gold dust will ride mighty easy in *my* saddlebags."

"It'll slow us down. We follow the plans to the letter," Slocum insisted. He began to doubt his wisdom in choosing Warren for the robbery. The man's plans were a bit too obvious. Slocum, Slick Bob, and Burnside would have to watch their backs every instant or Warren would end up with the entire plunder.

" 'Bout time," Slick Bob said, glancing up at the sky. The sun poked above the one-story buildings lining Federal Street. The bank stood, a stolid red brick structure with iron-barred windows, not a hundred yards distant. Their horses were tethered at the side of a bookstore, waiting for their riders to walk them to the front of the bank when the time was right.

"Any time now," Slocum agreed, snapping shut his brother Robert's watch. It was just shy of seven A.M. As he slipped the watch into his vest pocket, he heard the rattle of a freight wagon along the street. "There's Burnside." He shaded his eyes with his hand as he stared down the street. The slender young telegrapher made a big show of brushing dust from both sleeves, their signal that the gold had arrived at the Denver and Rio Grande terminal and would be deposited in the bank in a few minutes. They had argued over the best time to strike, and Slocum had prevailed.

The guards from the D&RG would dump the gold in the bank lobby and wait for a receipt before leaving. During this time, the bank guards would be more intent on moving their treasure trove into the vault than on protecting it.

Slocum insisted they wait for the railroad guards to leave before robbing the bank, even if it meant moving the gold back from the vault. Warren had wanted to burst in, six-shooters blazing. Slocum knew that only meant guards would die—and maybe one or two of the robbers. A week earlier, Slocum had opened an account in the bank, to see how the guards were armed. They carried sawed-off shotguns in addition to their six-guns. Slocum had never seen more than two guards in the bank at any time, but for a delivery of this size, there would be more. He felt it in his bones.

"Check the rear of the bank," Slocum ordered Slick Bob. The thin cowboy looked up, eyebrows arching like wiggly caterpillars. Slocum was glad he said nothing; he simply obeyed.

"You think he's gonna hold up or fold like a bad hand when the shooting starts?" Phil Warren pushed his hat back and dropped his feet to the boardwalk with a loud bang. His hand rested on the sweat-stained oak handle of his battered six-shooter, as if he wanted to gun down Slick Bob when he returned.

"Who do you mean?" Slocum paid Warren only scant

attention; he was more intent on the telegrapher. Burnside dusted off his arms again, signaling the arrival of the gold at the far end of Federal Street. Slocum turned in the other direction and saw a heavy wagon rattling to a halt in front of the bank, loaded with a half dozen men.

"Nothing to comment on out back, Slocum," came Slick Bob's report. He licked his lips when he saw the guards working to move a heavy iron box into the bank. "Didn't think they would carry it all in one strongbox, but then, I don't reckon its lock'll keep us out too long."

"Nope," Slocum said, slipping the leather thong off the hammer of his ebony-handled Colt Navy. He walked to the end of the boardwalk and caught up the reins of his horse. The animal shied, but Slocum kept it under control. He had wanted his horse of some months placed ten miles outside town, for the final leg of their escape. By the time they reached those horses, Denver would be boiling like an anthill with hot grease poured down it.

Slocum paused a moment as Warren pushed past him. He said in a low voice, so only Warren could hear, "No shooting unless they open up on us. This is a bank robbery, not a massacre."

"You worry too much, Slocum. You're like an old woman."

Slocum tugged on the reins and began walking his horse down the street. A small grin crept onto his lips when he saw the railroad guards pile into the wagon and rattle off, heading for some cafe for a late breakfast. Slocum dropped the reins over the top rail of a hitching post outside the bank, looked up the street to where Matt Burnside shifted nervously in the wagon, then pulled up a solid blue bandanna to hide his face.

"Let's get rich," Slocum said.

He drew his Colt and went to the front door. As he had suspected, the eager banker had closed it but had forgotten to lock it in his haste to move the gold into his vault. Slocum turned the knob, then kicked the door open.

"Get your hands up!" he shouted. Two guards stood with their backs to him. They half turned and saw they would never get the drop on Slocum. Both men dropped their shotguns and lifted their hands.

Slick Bob and Warren pushed past into the lobby, covering the tellers in their cages and the banker coming from the back office to see what the furor was. He opened his mouth, then gobbled like a turkey when Slick Bob pointed his six-shooter straight at the man's face.

"Wh-what do you want?" the banker finally got out.

"Get the damn gold from the vault," shouted Warren. "Get it or die on the spot!" Warren fired a round in the banker's direction.

Slocum stepped forward, wanting to slug his partner. If they fired for no reason, the guards and tellers might think they were dead no matter what they did. That made men do desperate things.

"You won't be hurt if you do what you're told," Slocum shouted. "Get the gold out here. Now!"

The banker gobbled some more, then said, "I can't lift that much. I wear a truss." His hand drifted toward his groin. Slocum moved to keep Warren from killing the man.

"He's not going for a gun. Not one that'll matter," Slocum said, moving nearer Warren.

"No gun, no," muttered the banker. He motioned in the direction of the vault. "The gold's back there in the safe. Don't kill me. Don't kill anybody!"

"You," Slocum said, pointing at one guard. "You and the banker man fetch the gold." He looked over his shoulder and saw Burnside reining to a halt outside, the wagon more than they needed for a hundred pounds of golden freight. Everything was going according to their plan—so far.

The guard and the grunting banker carried the strongbox from the vault. Slocum hesitated. He wanted to see what rested inside the iron box, to be sure they weren't carrying off the wrong container.

"Open it. Get the key and open it," Slocum ordered. He glanced away from the banker to Burnside, to see if the telegrapher was waiting patiently or might panic if his three partners didn't come running out of the bank right away with the gold. To Slocum's relief, Burnside didn't seem any more nervous now than he had when he pulled up.

"I don't have the key," the banker started. Slocum cocked his six-shooter and pointed it at the man. The sound of the Colt's hammer coming back snapped the banker's resolve. He fumbled in his vest pocket, pulled out a long, thin skeleton key, and applied it to the lock. It took several seconds for his trembling, clumsy hand to get the key into the lock.

"Check it," Slocum said, pushing Warren toward the box. He was getting antsy. This was taking too long. He wanted to load the gold into the wagon and keep the guards and tellers at gunpoint long enough to let Burnside drive off safely. Once in the increasingly busy Denver morning traffic, the wagon and telegrapher would simply vanish.

In two days' time, they would swing back to town and find Burnside at his job, working as if nothing had happened, and divvy up the gold. The hoopla over the robbery would have died, and although it would still be risky, they would stand a better chance of getting away scot-free.

"Looks like a hundred pounds of gold to me," Warren said. "And I see more back in that vault. There are bags of greenbacks, I bet."

"Wait!" Slocum called, but Warren had already vanished into the vault. He came out dragging two canvas bags laden with bank notes. This wasn't part of the robbery. Although it was lighter and easier to carry than the gold, Slocum had no liking for scrip. Most bartenders discounted a greenback by half or more. Coin was better than paper any day.

"I got 'em, Slocum," Warren said. Slocum almost pulled the trigger on the man when he named him. They had agreed not to use names. Now the law would know who one of the robbers was.

"Load the gold, then the greenbacks," Slocum ordered. He backed up and kept his gun trained on the men. The guards were beginning to exchange looks with one another and the banker. Slocum didn't have to be able to read their minds. The banker was promising them riches beyond their dreams of a dollar-a-day salary, if they would stop the robbers.

"On the floor, the lot of you," Slocum ordered, forcing them to move and break their determination. He kicked the shotguns to the far corner of the room and made sure their six-shooters joined them. He shot a quick look through the door at the wagon. Burnside helped Slick Bob and Warren load the gold. Warren came back for the canvas bags of paper money, and then all hell broke loose.

Slocum saw Burnside flip over the driver's seat and hit his head against the side of the wagon. Then a flight of bullets tore past the door. One broke the bank's plate glass window and sent shards flying through the lobby.

In the midst of the confusion, Slocum ducked outside to see what had gone wrong. He cursed under his breath. A Denver policeman had come over to the bank, either on business or out of simple curiosity about what was being loaded into the wagon. He had seen Slick Bob's mask, figured what was happening, and opened fire.

Slick Bob Durham hunkered down by the rear wagon wheel, firing methodically at the policeman. The officer had panicked at the sight of the robbery and foolishly emptied his six-shooter. Slick Bob kept him pinned down, but was bleeding from a wound in his left arm.

"You all right?" Slocum barked.

"Got a nick on my arm. Get worse'n this every time I go to a cheap barbershop. I don't know about our driver. He took a real dive when he got hit."

Slocum was pleased that Slick Bob, though wounded, hadn't blurted out names as Warren had. Slocum peered over the driver's box and saw Burnside struggling to sit up. A red flower blossomed squarely in the middle of his chest.

Though pale, the telegrapher seemed able to move.

"Can you get this rig out of here?" Slocum asked.

"I will," Burnside grated from between clenched teeth. "See you in two days."

"Wait, wait," shouted Warren. He dragged both canvas bags from the bank, leaving the guards untended. Warren heaved the bags into the rear of the wagon as Burnside got the team moving. But from inside the bank came the sound of shotgun hammers cocking.

"Get out of here now," Slocum shouted. "If we wait much longer, none of us will escape." He turned and fired point-blank at a guard in the doorway. The guard's scattergun blew a hole in the wood walkway at his feet, sending a rain of splinters into the air. The second barrel fired prematurely and blew off part of the door, blasting more wood fragments outward into the street. The guard staggered back, injured and off-balance, and blocked the second guard's exit. Slocum fired twice more through the door, driving the guards into the bank in search of cover. But Phil Warren calmly walked to the door, leveled his six-shooter, and fired a fatal round into the struggling guard's chest.

Rather than reloading, Slick Bob had gone for their horses and let the policeman slip off. The lawman ran screaming for help down the street, far beyond the range of a six-gun. Slocum considered making the shot, then forgot about it. His time would be better spent on the back of a galloping horse.

"Ride," he yelled, emptying his pistol through the window and door of the bank, to keep the guards inside for another few seconds. "Our lives depend on it!" He bent low and put his spurs to the reluctant horse's flanks, getting to a gallop as fast as he could. Beside him rode Slick Bob, clutching at his left arm; behind them, Phil Warren on a slower horse.

A hail of bullets from down Federal Street whined past Slocum's head. The lawman had fetched the marshal and three deputies, all with loaded guns and blood in their eyes.

2

"Ride, dammit, ride!" Slocum kept low over the neck of his horse, though the animal's gait was turning irregular and lather flowed freely from its flanks. Slocum knew he would have to shoot the horse when he dismounted, but if he didn't push the animal past its limits of endurance, he would be clapped into the Denver jail house and maybe marched up a gallows to swing.

He tried to remember what had happened once the policeman had blundered onto the robbery and started shooting. Slocum knew he might have killed one guard, the one who had fired both barrels of his shotgun into the boarding and door. Or maybe Warren had deliberately gunned the guard down. Stray bullets from all their six-shooters could have killed anyone inside the bank. Such a death wouldn't have been intentional, but the law didn't much care about that. The banker—or his family—and whoever owned the gold would be clamoring for blood. And they were likely to get it if Slocum didn't run the horse under him into the ground.

The horse began stumbling and almost threw him. He looked to his left and saw that Slick Bob's horse balked at running any farther. Ahead, Warren's mount kept up a steady gallop, the strongest of the three even if it had been slow out of the gate. Slocum didn't fault Warren for choosing the best of the horses for his own, but he did for the mistakes made during the robbery.

"You bleeding again?" he called to Durham. The man moved so that his left arm stayed pressed to his side, but Slocum had seen real injuries, and Slick Bob's didn't seem too serious. Still, he hadn't taken a good look at it. They had been too busy saving their hides from ventilation with more bullets.

"Just a trifle," the cowboy allowed. "Nothin' much to worry your head over. Now, *that's* what's worryin' me." Slick Bob lifted his chin and indicated the slowly vanishing Phil Warren. "He said he staked out fresh horses for us. I feel it in my bones that we're gonna have unwanted company soon." The thin cowboy tossed his head in the opposite direction, back toward Denver.

Slocum didn't bother answering. He had the same feeling. The law had come on them like flies to shit and weren't going to let them ride off without some pursuit. He hoped Matt Burnside had managed to get the wagon to a safe spot and stash the gold. He shook his head, wondering about the telegrapher's condition. The bullet Burnside had taken in the chest looked mighty bad.

"Can't gallop this nag another foot, Slocum," came Slick Bob's unhurried appraisal. "Let's hope Warren has our remuda close at hand."

Slocum reined back and walked alongside his partner. They didn't speak. They just kept riding, grimly determined to get the most distance from their horses as possible. The hot summer sun beat down on their backs, turning them sweaty and uncomfortable with trail dust.

"Now, lookee there," said Slick Bob. "Isn't that about the finest sight you ever laid eyes on?"

Slocum had to admit that it was. Just on the other side of a rise stood a stand of juniper. Waiting for them were three horses. Warren had already hopped off his tired horse and worked at saddling another, again the strongest of their reserve. Neither Slocum nor Durham much cared. Their horses wouldn't have gone another mile without dying beneath them.

"Didn't think you would be ready for us," Slick Bob said, the closest he was likely to get to complimenting Warren.

"Take a look at his arm while I saddle up," Slocum said to Warren, pointing at Slick Bob's bloody arm.

"I ain't no doctor. Do it yourself, if you've a mind." Warren swung into the saddle and waited impatiently, wanting to ride on but held back by Slocum and Durham.

Slocum ripped away Durham's checked shirtsleeve and sloshed water from his canteen on the wound. Slick Bob winced but said nothing. The groove was deep enough to have chewed away skin but not serious enough for anything more than a quick bandaging with Durham's bandanna.

"Thank you kindly, Slocum. My wing's almost good as new," Slick Bob lied. He walked around clucking like a chicken, then broke out laughing.

"What's so damn funny?" snapped Warren.

"We done it," Slick Bob said. "We robbed the goldanged bank, and we got away."

"You fool," snarled Warren, his cold blue eyes turning to fire. "That telegrapher's got our gold and two bags of greenbacks. We're not rich, and we haven't got away yet. There's a posse on our asses, sure as there's fire in the sky." His finger stabbed in the direction of the blazing Colorado sun.

"Reckon that's true, but we got away for the moment," Slick Bob said, settling into the saddle. "One thing at a time will suit me just fine."

Slocum didn't hear Warren's reply. The man savagely jerked at his reins and spurred his horse into a canter and then a gallop. Slick Bob tipped his hat in Slocum's direction, then took off at a dead run after Warren. Slocum finished cinching up his saddle and mounted. Slick Bob's optimism was out of line, as Warren's pessimism was. The robbery might have gone better, but it hadn't.

And they had ridden from town under their own power. If a posse were hot after them, they'd find their robbers gone in a cloud of dust. Slocum put his heels to the sorry swayback he had drawn for this leg of the escape and caught up with Slick Bob within minutes. His partner's horse was quickly developing a limp and would go lame if pushed too much harder.

"Slocum, you ride on. I'll bring up the rear. Just be sure to leave me a good horse for the last switch-off. Where you gonna head, north or south?"

"I'll ride along for a spell with you," Slocum said. "I know we didn't plan it this way, but it seems a good idea if we all get back to Denver now to see how Burnside's faring."

"I thought he was a goner when he flopped into the driver's box," Slick Bob said, nodding slowly in agreement. "Reckon I was wrong about the bullet killin' him 'cuz he got up and drove away as pretty as you please."

"He was hit bad," Slocum said, remembering more of the man's condition as other details faded. He was no longer fighting for his life. He could afford to take the time to reflect on Burnside's wound. "He was supposed to stash the gold under the telegrapher's office out at the rail yards till we got there. Don't know if he'll have the strength to move a hundred pounds of gold."

"I looked into the strongbox," Slick Bob said, a crooked grin on his face. "Never seen any filly as purty as that gold. It was all there in bullion. Mighty small little bars, not much bigger'n your finger, but that didn't matter to me. I loved it all."

This was the most Slocum had ever heard Slick Bob say at a time. He listened with only half an ear as they rode, pushing the horses to their limit, until Durham's horse pulled up lame. Slocum let the cowboy swing up behind him and then kept his nag trotting along the best he could. He wanted to know how close pursuit was, and how far ahead the third change of horses would be. But he had to content himself with thoughts of gold and getting away to spend it.

"There's the last place we switch off," Durham said. Warren had already reached the grassy area where the staked horses grazed. "Looks to me as if he's waiting for us."

Slocum grunted. He knew what Warren wanted, and he had come to the same decision. They had to return to Denver rather than pressing on, laying false trails and giving the posse a run for its money. Slocum hated to do this because of the risk, but they had no other choice. Matt Burnside had been seriously wounded. It wouldn't do having him taken to a doctor and telling some rheumy sawbones about the robbery. They would lose not only the gold but possibly their lives if the marshal had names to put on wanted posters.

This didn't bother Slocum unduly. He had enough posters with his likeness on them circulating throughout the West. Some were for crimes he had committed. Some weren't, but he had been included because it seemed possible he might have robbed a stage or railcar. The poster he feared the most carried a good picture of him and a hundred-dollar reward for a judge killing.

He had ridden with Quantrill and had protested the Lawrence, Kansas, massacre a bit too much. Bloody Bill Anderson had gut-shot him and left him for dead. It took Slocum many months to recover his strength and make his way back to Slocum's Stand in Georgia. By then the war was over, and the worst part of losing came home to roost. A carpetbagger judge had taken a fancy to the Slocum property and intended to use it for a stud farm.

Slocum's parents were dead, and his brother Robert had died during Pickett's Charge. The farm was all he had, and the judge claimed taxes hadn't been paid. He and a hired gun rode out one day to take the land, and John Slocum had ridden away that evening.

Two new graves, just beyond the springhouse, remained. And Slocum had been dogged ever since with federal judge-killing charges brought against him.

A new wanted poster saying he had robbed a Denver bank didn't frighten him one bit. But losing the gold from that robbery would do more than sorely vex him.

"Slocum, we got to—" began Warren. Slocum cut him off.

"We're circling around and heading back into town," Slocum said. "Burnside was hit pretty bad. We don't want the law nosing around and finding the gold."

"I told you it was a mistake trustin' a green kid. Why, he couldn't have been more'n twenty." Warren slumped forward, grumbling to himself.

Slocum and Slick Bob got to their horses. Slocum patted his mare's neck. She had carried him a goodly number of miles and had that much more in her. She had a strong heart and legs that kept moving, no matter how tired she might be. Slocum saddled the mare and looked around. It was hardly past noon, and they had already killed two horses under them. These mounts would have to last them back into Denver—and beyond.

Slocum hoped they wouldn't be riding hell-bent for leather, as they had to reach this point.

"A wide circle," he decided. "We get to the north of Denver and come in from the direction of Fort Collins. If anybody asks, we've been up in Wyoming doing some cowpunching."

"Why bother thinkin' up lies now?" complained Warren. "If anybody gets too nosy, just shoot 'em." He whipped out his six-shooter and pointed it at the sky.

"Leaving behind a trail of bodies is the last thing we want right now," Slocum said, growing tired of Phil Warren and his bloodthirsty ways. Slocum feared no man and had done his share of killing. Not all of it had been congenial, either. He hadn't ridden with Quantrill as any yellow-belly. But mostly he preferred to kill when the man was armed and facing him. He got the feeling that neither of those conditions meant much to Warren.

The feel of the six-shooter bucking in his hand, the sight of blood flowing and men dying—those were the important things to Slocum's bloodthirsty partner.

Slocum started on the trail back to Denver, heading north and then angling around to enter the town from an unexpected direction. It was past sundown when they rode along the Denver streets, passing through Larrimer Square with its saloons, dance halls, and whorehouses. Warren was obviously drawn to the clink of glasses and the bawdy laughter of wantons, but he had the good sense to stay with Slocum and Durham.

"They won't be looking for us here," Slocum said. "We can get right on out to the telegrapher's office and find Burnside. If we have to, we can jump a train headed south and be gone before midnight."

"With the gold," said Warren. "I ain't leavin' that snotty-nosed kid with the gold."

Slocum didn't reply. If Burnside had hidden the gold well, they could afford to let it be for a spell, then come back when the marshal no longer had visions of juicy reward money dancing in his head. Slocum hated to admit it, though, but Warren might be right. Burnside might not have done too good a job hiding the loot. That would mean they'd have to divvy it up and go their separate ways this very night.

"There's the rail yards," Slick Bob said. In the distance, a train whistle sounded. As if this nudged his memory, Slick Bob fumbled in his shirt pocket and pulled out the pine whistle he had been carving before the robbery. He licked his lips, put it to his mouth, and got a fair sound out of the whistle.

But he stopped playing "Dixie" when Warren complained.

"You go callin' attention to yourself with that song and we'll be knee-deep in deputies," Warren growled. Slocum suspected Phil Warren had fought for the Federals, and none too bravely. Hints he had dropped suggested a court-martial, maybe for thieving or even cowardice under fire. Slocum had no idea if Durham had fought for the Confederacy, but he thought it was a distinct possibility from the man's drawl. But Slocum had never asked and Durham had never volunteered any details.

"There's the telegrapher's office," Slocum said, pointing. The Western Union office was situated at the edge of the rail yards, surrounded by the trains from a half dozen different railroad lines. A lamp burned inside, and a dark figure hunched over the telegraph key. Even across the rail yards the *clackety-clackety-click* of the key could be heard distinctly. Slocum didn't know Morse code and wondered what the message might be.

"We can tether the horses there," Slick Bob said.

"You stay with 'em. Me and Slocum will see to the boy."

"I'm comin' with you," drawled Durham, a hint of steel in his voice.

"We'll all go," Slocum decided. He hadn't seen any lawmen as they rode into the yards, and the railroad detectives must have been out to dinner. The few men working were struggling to shift trains from one track to another for unloading.

They approached the telegrapher's office on foot. Slocum went in first, thumbs tucked into his gunbelt. He could reach the pistol in its cross-draw holster in a flash from this position, and yet he didn't appear outwardly menacing.

He blinked in the bright light from the lamp on the telegrapher's desk. An older man, missing most of his hair and a front tooth, stared up at Slocum with weak eyes. He adjusted his square glasses before clearing his throat.

"What can I do for you gents? There's the blanks for sendin' a telegraph, if that's your pleasure, and if it ain't, well, you can buy tickets for purt near anywhere the Burlington Northern, D&RG, or Union Pacific lines go, next door at the stationmaster's."

"We were looking for a friend. We . . . just rode into town from up north."

"Wyoming," cut in Slick Bob. "We were up there riding the range."

"We thought we'd look up an old friend by the name of Matt Burnside," Slocum went on, as if Durham hadn't interrupted. "Heard tell he worked here."

Behind him, Phil Warren grumbled under his breath about shooting the old man and getting on with the hunt for their gold.

"Well, he surely does, but he took ill this morning, right after all the hubbub."

"What caused the uproar?" Slocum asked, knowing what it was but playing to the hilt the part of a man newly arrived in Denver.

"There was a bank robbery. Those bandits got off with more than thirty thousand dollars' worth of gold and bank notes. Banker Longmire was fit to be tied." The telegrapher chuckled, then accurately spat into a cuspidor beside his desk. He waited for the brass to stop ringing before he went on.

"Matt came bursting into the office about the time of the robbery. Looked a mite peaked, he did."

"So?" pressed Slocum, growing as antsy as Warren to get the story out. "Is Burnside at home?"

"Can't rightly say. Maybe he took off with the posse. The federal marshal got his nose all out of joint, too. Folks are sayin' he can't keep the peace anymore. He's got a dozen deputies out patrollin' the streets, as if that'd do any good. Why lock the barn door when the horse has already been stole?"

"Is the marshal still in town?" Slocum asked the question as if it didn't much matter to him. He wanted to know if their decoying had worked.

"He's out west of town huntin' for the yahoos what robbed the bank. I don't think he'll find them." The telegrapher leaned over and looked across the top of his glasses, as if confiding in them. "Marshal Doaks cain't find his own arse with both hands *and* a posse."

"There's too many like him around," Slocum said in mock agreement. "But we're not too long in town, and we would like to find Matt."

"Well, as I was sayin', that's real strange. He blowed in here this morning and chased out Mrs. Elmendorff. She's the assistant telegrapher working mornings. He chased her out and sent four telegrams."

"Who'd he send them to?" demanded Slocum, an edge coming into his voice. The old man moved away, as if Slocum had stuck him with a pin.

"Can't say. But there was four of 'em. Then he left in a powerful hurry, and I ain't seen him the rest of the day."

The box above the key began clacking with an incoming telegram. The telegrapher turned to it, leaving Slocum and the others standing in front of the desk, wondering who Burnside had sent a telegram to.

Who he had sent *four* telegrams to.

3

"Where is that double-crossin' son of a bitch?" Phil Warren walked around outside the telegrapher's office, fuming mad. His fingers closed and opened over the butt of his six-shooter, and it looked as if he would draw down at any minute, firing at anything moving.

"We'll find him," Slocum said, sounding more confident than he felt. He worried more about the four telegrams. There wasn't any reason for Matt Burnside to come racing back to the telegraph station, send telegrams, then disappear like a ghost. Unless the young telegrapher had intended to double-cross them all the time.

Somehow, Slocum couldn't believe that. He was a good poker player and knew how to read men sitting across the table from him. Burnside was either one hell of a fine actor or had been playing straight.

"We can mosey around the yards and see if anybody's set eyes on the varmint," suggested Slick Bob Durham. For the first time, Slocum noticed a note of anger in the cowboy's voice. He opened and closed his folding knife, stopping only to drag his thumb along the keen edge now and again. It was unmistakable what he wanted to do with that knife.

If Matt Burnside had stolen their gold, Slocum wouldn't stop either of his partners if they wanted to shoot or stab the swindling sidewinder. But his gut told him something more than simple greed had caused Burnside to disappear. And the four telegrams. He couldn't keep from thinking about those four telegrams.

"Spread out," Slocum said. "Find what happened to him. If nothing turns up, meet back here." He eyed the telegrapher's station, knowing Burnside had intended to hide the gold beneath its wobbly foundations. Durham and Warren set off to question the men working in the Denver and Rio Grande side of the extensive yards, and Slocum dropped to his knees to peer under the flooring. The building had been moved several times, the last time to be dropped on top of a haphazard brick foundation. The muck beneath the floorboards wasn't too enticing, but the lure of gold drew Slocum under the shack. He wiggled around a bit, then lit a lucifer to see if the filth had been stirred up.

There was no way in hell Burnside could have hidden the strongbox and two greenback-filled canvas bags without leaving some trace. Save for a few rats and an alley cat hunting dinner, Slocum saw nothing to show that anyone had been under the station. He wiggled back out from under the telegrapher's station, brushed himself off, and looked around. A tumbledown wood plank building half the size of a small barn caught his eye. Its door hung on rusty hinges and had been pulled half off. As Slocum started for the storage shed, his other two partners returned.

"Nothing, Slocum," grumbled Slick Bob. "Nobody's seen him since this morning."

"Nobody'll fess up to seein' him," corrected Warren, in an even worse mood now. Slocum had seen the look in a man's eye when he wants to kill. Phil Warren came close to that point now. "I say we nab one of them and make 'em talk! The whole bunch are in cahoots!"

"See that?" Slocum pointed at the shed. "Tracks lead inside, just about the right width for that wagon Burnside drove."

"Gold!" whooped Slick Bob, racing forward. He pulled at the door, and it creaked open. He froze in the doorway. Warren and Slocum pushed close behind and stared into the shed.

"Don't have to look for Burnside anymore," Slocum observed. He slid past Durham, jumped into the wagon bed, and knelt by Burnside's body. Slocum rolled Burnside over and saw that the slug he had taken in the chest had done him in. After getting a closer look at the wound, Slocum wondered how the telegrapher had been able to live, much less move long enough to reach the rail yards.

"Don't see no gold," Warren said angrily. "The son of a bitch done us dirty, and now he can't pay for it!"

Slocum and Slick Bob carefully searched the shed and found that Warren was right. No gold. No greenbacks. Nothing. Slocum dropped behind the wagon and studied the depth of the wheel ruts. He shook his head as he stood.

"The gold wasn't in the wagon, not when he drove it in. Can't say what happened to the team or the gold."

"Guards," hissed Slick Bob, peering out the shed door. "A half dozen of them, all armed with clubs. They're after two guys tryin' to jump a train."

"We're not going to find the gold here," Slocum said, lost in thought. The key to the gold lay in those four telegrams, but for the life of him, Slocum couldn't figure who Burnside had wired. He climbed into the saddle and rode slowly from the rail yards. He wasn't going to give up.

"What do we do now? Get the hell out of Denver?" Slick Bob was as down in the mouth as Slocum had ever seen him. He wasn't feeling too sprightly himself, but he had more determination. Burnside couldn't have gotten far with the gold in his condition, not upping and dying within hours of the robbery. Slocum decided Burnside had had less than three hours to stash the gold before expiring.

"We'll go back to the hotel and think on this a spell," Slocum said. Surprise blossomed on Slick Bob and Warren's faces.

"Have you gone plumb loco, Slocum?" demanded Slick Bob. "The whole danged town's buzzing with the robbery."

"Except for one slip," Slocum said, glaring at Warren, "nobody has any idea who pulled the robbery. You can ride on out, if you like. I'm staying to find the gold."

"I ain't leavin'," declared Warren, looking suspiciously at Slocum, as if he had had something to do with hiding the gold.

"I'm in, too," Durham decided. "Looks like we're puttin' our necks in a noose, but I'm stayin'."

They rode slowly through the bustling nighttime Denver streets until they reached their hotel. They stabled their horses down the street and went in. Slocum had paid for a week on his room and still had two days left. He saw no reason to waste the money. A hot bath, a steak in the hotel's cafe, and a night's sleep in a clean bed might improve his outlook.

Figuring what Matt Burnside had done with the loot from the robbery would go a tad farther in improving his disposition.

"Key," he asked of the room clerk. The man jumped as if unexpectedly branded. He leapt from his chair and came to the counter.

"Wasn't expecting to see you so early, Mr. Johnson," the clerk said, giving the name Slocum had assumed to rent the room. "You either, Mr. Smith, Mr. Harris." The clerk nodded in the direction of the other two. Slocum tried to remember which name Warren had assumed and couldn't. Summer names were slippery, as easy to confuse as two rattlers in a burlap bag.

The clerk reached for the keys to the men's rooms. Slocum's eyes narrowed when he saw a telegram next to each one. The clerk handed over the yellow envelopes with the keys.

"You men certainly are popular, each of you getting a telegram like that."

Slocum snatched the flimsy envelope from the clerk and ripped it open. He turned over the sheet to be sure nothing more was written on it than the two words on the front: "Hidden Compartment."

"What's yours say?" he asked Durham.

Slick Bob held out the sheet, confirming what Slocum had suspected. Durham couldn't read. This wasn't much of a lack since all his telegram said was "D&RG".

"Yours?" asked Slocum. Phil Warren held his close to his chest, as if he had been dealt a royal flush, but he reluctantly showed it when he saw the other two men's messages. His read, "Freight Car."

"What do you make of it, Slocum?" Slick Bob sat in a chair at the far corner of the lobby, rustling the yellow paper nervously. "I reckon Burnside sent these, but what do they mean?"

"He sent each of us a part of where he stashed the gold," Slocum said.

"So he hid the gold in a Denver and Rio Grande freight car with a hidden compartment?" Warren snorted in disgust. "There must be hundreds of cars in that damn yard, since it's shared by all the railroads coming into Denver. How do we know which freight car? And how do we know it's still even in the yards? Trains come and go all the time, and it's been a goodly eighteen hours since the robbery."

"We can't know which one," Slocum said, turning everything he had found out over in his head. A piece was missing, and neither of his partners had caught on to what it was. The fourth telegram had to specify which freight car—but who had received that message?

"To hell with it," exclaimed Warren. "I'm gettin' out of this town before it's too late."

"What?" Slocum looked at his partner, startled at Warren's sudden change of heart.

"You heard me. I'm cuttin' out of here while I can. You two find the gold, it's yours. Better to be broke and free than caged up again. I couldn't stand that, not for even one more day." Warren never glanced back as he stormed from the hotel lobby. The clerk watched curiously as Warren slammed the door, then he went back to whatever chores he had behind the counter.

"Reckon that leaves us with a fifty-fifty split, Slocum." Slick Bob took off his Stetson and scratched his balding head. "But then half of nothin' ain't much, is it?"

"No, it's not," Slocum said. "I've got a few ideas that might turn it into a bit more, though."

"An idea like who got that fourth telegram?" Slick Bob smiled from ear to ear. "Warren never was much for thinkin' things through. That man might be quick with his six-shooter, but he's mighty slow where it counts." Durham tapped the side of his head.

"Let's get some chow and check out a few freight cars—and the telegrapher's record book," Slocum said.

"My thoughts exactly."

The two went their separate ways long enough for Slocum to take his bath and draw a straight razor across his face, to cut through his day-old beard, then they met again in the lobby. Slocum felt as if he could whip his weight in wildcats and was confident they could track down the elusive fourth telegram.

"I been outside, sitting and listenin'," Slick Bob Durham said. Slocum saw that the man hadn't taken the time to clean up any. He still had a day's trail dust on him and a three-day growth of beard that would probably still be there in the morning. "The whole town's riled about the robbery."

"More than having the gold stolen?" Slocum heard the edge in Slick Bob's voice.

"The guard didn't make it. Took two bullets, one in the belly and the other smack-dab in the center of his face. Thinking back on it, I might have been the one who drilled him with the second bullet."

"It doesn't matter who shot him," Slocum said, not sure if he was responsible. Or even Phil Warren. "The way the lead was flying, it could have been any of us." He chewed at his lower lip, thinking Warren might have the right idea. Staying to unearth the gold wasn't too smart. The bank wouldn't cotton much to losing the gold, but the whole town got in an uproar over a killing.

"Reward's not too big, but it might entice Warren," Slick Bob went on. "Two hundred dollars to the man who puts us into the Denver jail."

"Is the marshal still out hunting for us?"

"That might be the only bright spot," Slick Bob said. "From what I hear, he might be gone a month, or until somebody sends out a search party for him. Marshal Doaks might do good breakin' up bar fights, but on the trail, the man is a greenhorn."

"We got freight cars to look at," Slocum said, coming to a decision. If the marshal and any number of his deputies followed a cold trail, that gave them an added chance for finding the gold and simply vanishing. To the east lay Kansas and Nebraska, not Slocum's favorite territories, but St. Louis could be a whale of a lot more interesting with enough gold coin jingling in his pockets.

They returned to the freight yards, arriving just after midnight. A freight train rumbled and clanked on its way south. Slocum worried that one of those cars held the secret niche loaded with his gold. If one of them did, it was lost to him.

"The dispatcher knows the numbers on the cars," Slick Bob said, following the same line of thought. "We get the right number, we can find where the car went."

"Trains wreck all the time," Slocum said, a touch of pessimism hitting him now. "Imagine all that gold and those greenbacks scattered across the Colorado countryside." He dismounted to the side of the telegrapher's shack. It wasn't a picture he wanted to keep in his head for too long. It might give him nightmares.

"We got to be logical about this. That young Burnside looked to be the kind who worked more in his head than with his hands," said Slick Bob. "All we got to do is figure like he would."

"He was hurt. He couldn't have moved the gold around too much," Slocum said, trying to imagine what Matt Burnside had gone through when he arrived with the gold in the wagon bed. "The wagon must have slipped alongside the freight car." Slocum stopped and frowned.

"I was thinkin' the same thing, Slocum. How'd a young sprout like our Mr. Burnside know of a secret cranny in any boxcar?"

"He must have been doing more than pounding away at the key in there." Slocum peered through a dirty window at a woman sitting with a far-off look in her eye as she scribbled down an incoming wire.

"Wouldn't take more than a few pounds of freight smuggled here and there to give him more than a telegrapher's salary to live on," Slick Bob observed. "You reckon that old lady knows anything about it?"

"I want to check the boxcars closest to the telegrapher's shack before we go poking around and asking her," Slocum said. The fewer people who knew of their interest in Matt Burnside, the better. A glance toward the decrepit storage shed showed that the young telegrapher's body hadn't been discovered yet.

Slocum and Slick Bob Durham searched the freight cars nearest the telegrapher's station to no avail. Slocum was sitting with his legs dangling out an open door when he heard the crunch of boots on cinders.

His hand drifted toward his Colt Navy, but he didn't draw. A conductor carrying a lantern walked by, only seeing Slocum at the last second.

"What you doin' in there? You get on out now, you hear?" The conductor's voice carried in the still morning air. "You pay for a ticket like real folks."

"I was hunting for a friend. Somebody told me I could find him here," Slocum said. "Maybe you know him. Matt Burnside."

"The kid who pounds the key in the telegraph office? Sure, I know him. What's your business with him?"

"Family business," Slocum said.

"You don't look like family to me." The conductor moved closer, holding up the lantern. "No, sir, you don't look like family at all."

"I'm not related. I have news of his brother, though," Slocum said, fishing for any information he could get from the conductor.

In the distance a whistle blew twice, indicating a train prepared to pull out. The conductor swung the lantern around, torn between duty and interrogating Slocum. Duty and a departing train won out.

"You go on over to the office and talk to Mrs. Elmendorff. I don't have time to deal with you." The conductor started off, then halted and shot back over his shoulder, "Burnside don't have a brother."

Slocum shrugged, then jumped to the ground. He knew his time in the yard had run out. The conductor would find one of the roving gangs of detectives and send them after the stranger who didn't know squat about a man he claimed as a friend.

He walked quickly toward the telegrapher's office, pausing only when Durham met him. "Couldn't find anything, Slocum," the cowboy lamented. "You?"

"Found out that Burnside didn't have a brother." Slocum didn't bother explaining the cryptic comment. He pushed Slick Bob into deeper shadow and waited when they saw the woman telegrapher named Mrs. Elmendorff come to the door and look around.

"What's she doing?" whispered Slick Bob.

"Leaving for a few minutes," Slocum said, a grin coming to his lips. The telegrapher hurried down the steps and vanished into the night. "Answering a call of nature, maybe."

"She looks to be the kind who has a man waiting for her," said Slick Bob. "She's a mite old, but I could enjoy a woman like that."

Slocum's mind wasn't on women as he hurried up the steps and into the telegrapher's office. The mechanism clattered and clicked with the long and short bursts that spoke to the men and women who knew Morse code. Slocum ignored the chatter. He slid into the hard chair in front of the key and looked around, not sure what he sought.

He reached for a thick book stuffed with loose papers and pulled it out. As he opened it, his heart almost exploded.

"Lookee there," said Slick Bob, peering over his shoulder. "Are those copies of the telegrams?"

"Not copies," Slocum said, certain now that Durham couldn't read a lick. "These tell who got the telegrams." He ran his finger down the list until he came to four shaky entries.

"Burnside must have been in a bad way if that's his handwriting," Durham said. "What'd he write? I can't make it out it's so wobbly."

"Telegrams to Harris, Johnson, and Smith—"

"Them's our names," said Durham, getting excited.

"He sent them to the hotel. And there's the fourth." Slocum's finger stabbed down on the last entry Matt Burnside had made before sending the telegrams.

The fourth had been sent to PB in Fort Collins.

4

"That's all?" Slick Bob Durham backed away and spat. He missed the cuspidor by inches and spattered tobacco juice on the floor. The thick gob began draining through the wide cracks in the boards, making Slocum glad he had checked for the gold underneath the shack before they'd discovered the recipient of the fourth telegram.

"How many men with the initials PB can there be in Fort Collins?" Slocum asked. "We go up and—" He held out his hand to silence Slick Bob when he heard angry voices outside.

". . . around somewhere," came a gravelly voice. "The conductor on the southbound told me, and I been huntin' for ten minutes. Josh over there found two horses, so he might have a partner."

"You think this is the bank robber?" came a second voice, grating and angry.

"Don't go gettin' your dander up, Deputy."

"Dammit, that was my brother who got murdered at the bank. I'm not letting any back-shooting bank robber walk away if I got him in my sights!"

Slocum pushed out of the chair and went to the station window. The dirty pane of glass shielded him a mite. Not ten feet away stood a half dozen men. Five huddled

together. He took them to be the railroad guards patrolling
the yard to keep unwanted passengers from riding for free
in the freight cars. The sixth man turned slightly, sending
reflections off a badge. Slocum ducked back to keep the
man from seeing him.

"We're trapped in here, Slocum." Durham started for
the door and his gun at the same time. Slocum caught
his forearm and kept him from drawing.

"We can't fight all of them. If we stay put, we might ride
this out."

"Bullshit!" whispered Slick Bob. "We're trapped, and
they're gonna stretch our necks. You heard him. That's the
dead guard's *brother*. He's not interested in any reward. He
wants our blood!"

"He's just guessing that we might be the bank robbers.
There's nothing to tie us in."

". . . overheard one name. Slocum. Did the conductor
mention that name?" asked the deputy. Slocum's heart rose
and caught in his throat. Warren's stupid blunder might
cost him his life. He had heard stories about Canon City
Penitentiary, and he didn't much like the notion of spending
any time there. He knew he wouldn't have even that galling
choice if the deputy caught up with him.

"We fight," Slick Bob said, pulling his six-shooter.

"We can get out of here without being seen. Let them
go their way." Even as Slocum spoke, the woman telegrapher returned. She went to talk with the railroad guards a
moment, then turned and pointed. Slocum knew either he
or Durham had cast a shadow. The guards hadn't thought
anything about it, believing the telegrapher was at her work.
Now they knew different, and they were coming to find out
who was in the office.

Slocum glanced up and saw that the tar-paper roof was
weak in places, but there wasn't time to poke and prod
and find just the right spot to scramble onto it. Even if
they had had the time, that would have been a precarious
escape route. They would have been exposed if they came

out on the wrong side of the pitched roof.

"The floor. Find a loose board," Slocum said urgently to Slick Bob. Slocum dropped and pried loose a board with his fingers. The cowboy found a second board, giving them barely enough room to drop below the flooring and into the muck below.

"Damn you, Slocum. I'll never be clean again," complained Slick Bob.

"We get the gold, we can take all the baths we want," Slocum said, snaking his way toward the far side of the telegrapher's shack. He poked his head through a break in the brick foundation, then pushed on out into the cold morning air. The morning star shone down brightly, making Slocum feel like an actor with a spotlight focused on him. The railroad guards and deputy had stormed into the office and were crashing about.

If they didn't escape now, they never would.

"Come on," he said, grabbing Slick Bob's arm and pulling the man through the crack. If the cowboy closed one eye, he'd look like a needle, but he was having a devil of a time getting out from under the telegraph office. Slocum tugged again and Slick Bob came free.

"There's no need to get to our horses. They found them. They might have a trap set, or at least a couple guards," Slocum said. He didn't want to abandon his mare or gear, but getting away was more important than anything riding in or under his saddlebags.

As he started walking, his boots made sucking sounds. He tried to move faster, but the noise had drawn unwanted attention.

"Hey, there, stop! You two owlhoots! Stop!"

Slocum ducked as a bullet narrowly missed his head. He ducked and began running for all he was worth, Slick Bob at his side. They dove under a boxcar, rolled, and came out on the far side of the tracks. The entire yard was coming alive, everyone's attention turning toward them. The gunshots and loud cries to halt would stop them quick if they didn't think of something.

"Let's split up. One of us might get away," suggested Durham. "I'll try to circle round and come up on them from the side. If I have to, I can ventilate one or two of 'em."

"Just get away," Slocum said, already turning to run away from the boxcar. More bullets kicked up cinders around him, but the moonless night worked in his favor at the moment. Occasional clouds drifted through the sky, cutting some of the brilliant starlight and giving him the chance to dive headfirst into an open boxcar. He swung about and lay prone on the rough planking, his cocked Colt Navy pointing out the open door. If anyone had stuck up his head, Slocum would have blown it off.

But the sounds of pursuit diminished as the railroad guards went in a different direction. Slocum breathed a sigh of relief for saving his own hide, though he knew this meant the others had found Slick Bob Durham's trail and taken out after him. The cowboy was a decent enough tracker. Slocum reckoned Slick Bob could get away, given just a smidgen of luck.

As Slocum got to his feet, the car lurched and threw him back down. He rolled easily and came up with his back against the rear wall. The steel wheels clattered beneath the car as it built up speed. Slocum made his way back to the door and peered ahead. The engine puffed hard, huge plumes of black smoke reaching into the early morning sky. This car and dozens hooked to it were being moved.

Slocum started to jump from the boxcar and stopped when he saw a tight knot of guards. In the midst of the group stood the deputy, an expression of utter rage on his face. Slocum ducked back into the boxcar, hoping he hadn't been seen.

The bullet ripping off a chunk of wood next to his head told him the deputy had spotted him. Slocum stumbled to the far side of the jerking boxcar and tried to force open the other door. It was secured on the outside. Slocum whirled around, his six-gun leveled. He fired just as the deputy's hat poked past the open door.

The floppy-brimmed hat went flying, but Slocum knew he hadn't even scratched the lawman with his round. He waited for a second chance, but the train built up enough speed to outrace even the most determined deputy. Slocum settled down and watched as the outskirts of Denver whipped past. Ten minutes out of town he considered jumping off, then stopped as he prepared to do so.

The engine chugged along at a brisk clip, and Slocum noticed that the train was heading north. He settled down, legs hanging over the edge of the boxcar, railroad ties flashing by underneath his boots. He looked back and knew that returning to Denver would be the same as a death sentence. He had overheard enough to know that the deputy carried a personal grudge and was more likely to shoot first than arrest.

Even if he stood trial, Slocum knew he might swing, even if Warren was the one who had cut down the bank guard. There wasn't anything for him in Denver, but the Burlington Northern went toward Wyoming and Montana.

Through Fort Collins. Where someone with the initials P.B. had received a telegram giving the final clue needed to find the gold. Slocum settled down and watched the countryside roll by. He hadn't planned his escape, but it worked out better than he could have hoped. When he tired of watching the land rush past, he hiked his feet into the boxcar and lay back, trying to get comfortable. Somehow, in spite of the noise and uneven rattle of the steel wheels under him, he managed to sleep.

He came awake with a start, hand tightening around the butt of his six-shooter when the train slowed. Slocum scrambled to the open door and saw a small town ahead.

"Fort Collins," he said, smiling crookedly. He waited for a tight curve that forced the engine to slow, then he jumped off. Even then, he rolled and fetched up hard against a signpost. Cursing, he rubbed his bruised ribs and pulled himself to his feet. The walk into town made his feet ache but was worth it. Getting caught by railroad detectives in the Burlington Northern yards would have been stupid.

His belly was growling from lack of food and he could hardly stay awake from lack of sleep when he reached the first group of buildings, at the outskirts of town. Fort Collins didn't look any different from a hundred other places Slocum had seen. He checked his pockets and found two greenbacks folded tightly. At a small restaurant, he ordered a stack of flapjacks, bacon, and enough black coffee to drown in. He finished off the meal and felt better.

"Anything else?" asked the waiter, seeing how Slocum had cleaned his plate down to the last drop of molasses.

"Need to send a telegram. Where's the telegraph office?"

The waiter shrugged and made a vague gesture toward the center of town. "Western Union's office is next to the railroad station. You ought to have seen it when you got in."

"What makes you think I came in on the train?" Slocum sat up straighter.

"You ain't one of them Denver lawmen? A passel of them arrived maybe a half hour back. Mistook you for one of them."

"I rode into town," Slocum lied. It had taken him more than an hour to walk in from where he'd jumped off the train. He tried to remember if another train had raced by afterward. He thought one might have, but he couldn't be sure, since he had been more intent on reaching Fort Collins than in monitoring railroad traffic.

If the deputy had commandeered another train, one without a long line of boxcars behind it, he could have arrived at just about the same time as the train Slocum had stowed away on.

"Don't get many folks coming through here," the waiter said, taking Slocum's greenback with some distaste. He fumbled in his dirty apron pocket and slowly counted out the change, leaving it on the edge of the table. Slocum pushed it toward him for a tip. The information that the deputy had arrived, maybe with a small posse, merited some reward.

"Thanks," the waiter said dryly, staring at the bit piece left on the table.

Slocum settled his gunbelt around his waist and stood in the restaurant door, carefully studying the street for unusual activity. Fort Collins was small, and a few additional lawmen would stand out as the townspeople stared at them. Wherever the deputy hunted, it wasn't along Fort Collins's main street. Walking slowly and keeping his eyes open, Slocum made his way toward the telegraph office.

He stopped and peered inside. His hand twitched when he saw the Denver deputy talking with the telegrapher. Backing off, Slocum ducked into an alley and hunkered down behind a rain barrel. The click of boot heels on the wood planking in front of the telegraph office caused Slocum to tense. He slid his Colt Navy from its holster and waited.

"You find anything?" the deputy called. Slocum peered around the barrel and saw the Denver lawman standing in the mouth of the alley, but his attention turned toward another man, crossing the dusty main street.

"Can't say I did, Tom. Nobody in town's seen that owlhoot."

"He's here somewhere. He got on that train for some reason more than escaping me." The deputy's fingers drummed on the handle of his six-shooter. "I can *smell* him he's so close. Don't give up."

"Tom, you think the marshal'll take kindly to us comin' all the way up here? Takin' over that train like you did wasn't too smart. The stationmaster back in Denver said—"

"I don't give a tinker's damn what he said," snapped the deputy. "Those sonsabitches killed my brother. They're not gettin' by with it. I swear, they aren't."

"Both got away, Tom," the other lawman said softly.

"One got away. I know the other one's around Fort

Collins. Find him, dammit. Find him!"

The deputy stalked off, heading down the street toward the restaurant where Slocum had eaten breakfast. Time was running out. When the lawman talked to the waiter, there would be hell to pay. Slocum slid his six-gun back into his holster and went directly into the telegraph office. He had to find what he needed and get out of Fort Collins as fast as possible.

The telegrapher looked up from under his green eye-shade. He frowned, thinking Slocum was another interruption and not more business. "What can I do for you?" he asked testily.

"I need to send a telegram," Slocum said. The telegrapher brightened.

"That's about the best news I've had all morning. Nothing but those big city lawmen coming through here, throwing their weight around, accusing me of knowing things I don't." The man pushed his eyeshade back and lifted his pencil to take Slocum's message. When Slocum didn't start dictating, he looked up. "Go on. Tell me what you want sent."

"I want this to be private," Slocum said.

"I don't tell anybody what's in any telegram sent," the man said. "And I *have* to know what's in the message since I'm sending it. There's no way I can put it into code if I don't know what you want sent."

"I realize that," Slocum said. He edged closer, peering at the man's desktop. The key's base had been nailed down to the edge of the desk. Beside it stood the larger box that relayed incoming messages. Two closed folders neatly tucked into a case beside the desk completed the picture of neatness.

"Well, get on with it. I don't have all day, thanks to those nosy lawmen."

"What did they want?"

"Who knows? They asked about a stranger in town." The way the man's face changed told Slocum that he had only a few seconds before the telegrapher began to ask questions Slocum didn't want to answer.

"I was supposed to pick up a telegram here sent from down in Denver," Slocum said, thinking fast.

"What name?" The telegrapher didn't look convinced, and Slocum saw the questions forming in the man's head. Slocum wanted to turn and look behind him to see if the deputy had come up on him. But he didn't. Any such glance would have confirmed the telegrapher's growing concerns.

"It'd be addressed by my initials. PB."

"I remember that wire," the telegrapher said. "I took it, but it wasn't for anybody here in town. It was marked for relay."

"Relay?"

"It came in from the Denver office for relay back south. I remember that because it's unusual for an operator to ask for a relay from an out-of-the-way station like Fort Collins."

"You're not on the main telegraph line?"

"Sure we are, going north. Why send a wire here when it's meant for the other direction?"

"Maybe it got mixed up. It was meant for me. PB." Slocum tried to figure out why Burnside had asked for a relay. The only thing he could think was that Burnside didn't wanted the recipient identified easily. And he hadn't been. Slocum still had no idea who held the final piece of the puzzle telling where the gold was hidden.

"No mix-up. I did what was requested," the clerk said, a smug expression on his face.

"Well, it shouldn't have been re-sent. What was the message?"

"Can't tell you that," the clerk said, turning cautious again. Memories of the deputy's questions returned.

"You mean I have to go down to Pueblo to get a telegram sent to me here?" Slocum asked, probing for any information.

"It wasn't sent to Pueblo. It was sent to Manitou Springs."

The telegrapher snapped his mouth shut, aware that he had said the wrong thing. "What's your name? Maybe I can find a copy of the telegram and get it to you. After lunch."

Slocum knew the man was lying through his teeth. He wanted time to find the deputy and tell him about the stranger asking after a telegram.

"You don't have a copy of the telegram," Slocum said rather than asked. "You relayed the wire and then tossed out your notes."

"Didn't need to make any," the telegrapher said, turning more frightened by the minute. "It came in and I relayed it at the same time. I'm good. I can relay faster than anyone else along the line."

Slocum left the telegraph office. The mysterious PB was southwest of Denver, not up in Fort Collins. But he had to be getting closer. As nervous as the clerk had been, he would have blurted out still another relay notice if there'd been one.

PB was in Manitou Springs, at the base of Pikes Peak. Slocum had started toward the railroad station when he heard the sound of a six-shooter's hammer cocking behind him.

5

"Who are you?" The question made Slocum reconsider turning and trying to get his Colt Navy in action before the deputy shot him down like a dog.

"Depends on who's asking," Slocum said. He turned slowly, hands out at his sides, well away from his six-shooter. The deputy was edgy enough without Slocum making him trigger-happy.

Slocum let out a deep breath when he saw that it wasn't the deputy from Denver behind him. The man wore a tarnished badge, but from the way the sunlight glinted off it, Slocum knew that this was a sheriff.

"You just come in on the train?"

"The special from Denver," lied Slocum. "I came up with the deputy. Maybe you've met him. Works with Marshal Doaks. His name's Tom." Slocum hoped this sheriff, an old man looking for retirement rather than a gunfight, could be bluffed. Mention of the deputy's first name went a way toward lulling the sheriff's suspicions.

"Reckon I have. You having any luck finding that bank robber?" The sheriff put his six-gun back into its holster. Slocum wondered if this were the first time the gun had been pulled for anything other than cleaning. The sheriff bordered on being an antique, just like the black-powder

Remington 1858 Army he sported as a sidearm.

"No luck. I got to head back real quick on other business. When's the next train?"

"That's an express barreling down the tracks right now," the sheriff told him. "Don't stop here, though. But it does go on into Denver, if you could get aboard."

"Does it slow down enough to get aboard?" asked Slocum, judging his chances of dying trying to jump the train as being better than staying in Fort Collins for even another ten minutes.

"Come on into the station. Might be able to signal it to slow down a mite, if this is important." The sheriff shuffled past him and into the station, not bothering to give Slocum a second glance. Slocum's luck had held again.

"Johnny, is there any chance of getting the express to slow up for this gent? He needs to get on back to Denver."

The stationmaster looked up from his newspaper, checked the regulator clock ticking mournfully on the wall, then half stood and peered out the window, down the tracks. He shook his head and went back to reading.

"Reckon not," the sheriff said.

"He's a talkative son of a buck, isn't he?" Slocum stared at the stationmaster.

"When he has to be. You can get a ticket on the regularly scheduled train in a couple hours."

"Too late," Slocum said. "Tom is going to be mighty upset if I don't tend to business. The marshal's getting back to town and needs some news we turned up."

"A couple hours won't matter much. Or send a telegram. You was just comin' out of the office when I found you. Good luck, young fella." The sheriff shuffled out of the station, making his rounds of a sleepy Fort Collins. Slocum saw that the stationmaster paid him no attention as he went out onto the platform. The express rattled closer, but Slocum noticed that it was slowing to hook a canvas bag stuffed with mail at the far end of the platform. The door into the mail car stood open, and the mail clerk inside waited for the pickup.

Slocum had only a split second to make his decision. As the train flashed by and the hook snared the mailbag, he jumped. Quick reflexes and a good eye helped him land in a heap in the center of the mail car floor. A second after he hit, the mailbag slid down a rod and crashed next to him. The mail clerk was even slower to respond, but when he did, he was outraged.

"Why'd you go and do a damn fool thing like that? You coulda knocked the bag off. The letters woulda been scattered across the countryside!"

"Sorry," Slocum said, sitting up and brushing himself off. He had crawled in muck and ridden in a boxcar and spent the better part of the past twenty-four hours dodging the law. He wasn't up to arguing with a wet-behind-the-ears mail clerk about jumping aboard the express to Denver. "They told me this was the only way I could get aboard."

"It's nonstop," the clerk muttered, his anger dying when he saw Slocum, and the ebony-handled Colt Navy hanging at his left side. "You a lawman?"

Slocum didn't answer directly. "That was some dustup in Denver, wasn't it?"

He had hit the nail on the head. The clerk nodded agreement. "We heard about the robbery all the way up in Wyoming. Have you caught the men who done it?" The clerk's face lit up, as he thought he was in the presence of some highfalutin lawman. Slocum kept from laughing only through iron will.

"Not yet, but the marshal's due back. He lit out after the robbers."

"What are you doin' up here? The gold came from the Denver and Rio Grande, not us. Not the Burlington line."

"Robbers can run to the damnedest places," Slocum said, flopping down on a stack of mailbags. They weren't as comfortable a bed as he'd known, but they were a sight better than bare floor. "Mind if I catch some shuteye until we get back to Denver?"

"No, go on. I got work to do. If you'd just sleep over there, I'd appreciate it. Got to sort the mail." The clerk pointed wistfully to a small cot stashed behind a desk. Slocum thanked the man and dropped onto the cot, knowing he was taking the man's bed and not caring. He slept heavily until the train lurched, almost throwing him onto the floor.

"What's going on?" Slocum boiled up and off the cot, six-shooter in hand.

"Can't rightly say," the clerk admitted. He swung out the door of the mail car and squinted ahead. "Best I can tell, there's a couple railroad ties on the tracks. We're being stopped!"

"Train robbery?" Slocum moved to the door and stared. From the way the men went about their business, this was no robbery. A posse had decided he was on the train. He cursed his bad luck. Either the Fort Collins sheriff had mentioned him to the deputy or the telegrapher had told the lawman about his strange visitor. Either way, a wire had been sent back to Denver to stop the train and arrest him.

"Much obliged for the use of the cot," Slocum said, swinging up the side and getting to the top of the train. From his vantage point he saw that the lawmen had stopped the train just shy of the rail yard. Engines moving along half a dozen different tracks puffed and chugged back and forth through the maze of switches.

Slocum began walking toward the rear of the train, where a conductor was waving at him. He got to the next to last car and then climbed down the iron rung ladder on the side away from the lawmen. He was close enough to the yards that he hoped he could lose himself—and that was the reason the deputies had stopped the train before it pulled into the station. He could have escaped more easily there.

"There he goes. Stop him, stop him!" cried the conductor.

Bullets began kicking up dirt and cinders all around Slocum. He ducked and ran even faster, dodging and trying to find some cover. The stretch he sprinted across afforded no hiding places. But ahead he saw the caboose of another train, building up steam to pull out of the yards. He got close enough to close his fingers around the back railing, then stumbled and fell facedown onto the tracks. The train kept moving, and he knew he'd lost his chance.

"After him. Get him. He's the one Tom wants. I can feel it in my bones!" A new round of firing caused Slocum to roll over the tracks, using one steel rail as scanty protection. When a bullet ricocheted off the steel inches from his face, Slocum knew he had to run again. But where?

A shorter train, only ten cars and none of them freight cars, had been pulled into a siding. Slocum made a beeline for the train, hoping it would pull out when the freight train rumbled far enough down the line. He hit the ground, rolled beneath a fancy passenger car, and came out on the far side. A quick glance around told him he had to risk hiding inside the Pullman car. The open space between him and the main section of rail yards was too great.

A single bullet could fly faster than he ever could run.

"Stop!" came the distant shout. The entire posse was after him now. Slocum swung onto the fourth car's rear platform and tried the door. Locked. He quickly stepped to the fifth car's door and tried it. The door came open so easily he almost tumbled. He whirled about, slammed the door, and slid the simple bolt lock into place. Only then did he look around to see where he had taken refuge.

He let out a low whistle at such opulence. Slocum had seen the Union Club in San Francisco and any of a dozen Mississippi riverboats that matched the richly cut red velvet drapes, the ornately woven Persian rug on the floor, and the gilt-edged lamps and other furnishings. He had seen the like but never in a railway car.

He had started for the rear partition when he heard noises inside a narrow, long room off to one side. He reached for the doorknob just as the door opened. Slocum wasn't sure who was more surprised.

The woman hadn't expected to see a grimy, desperate owlhoot like John Slocum standing in the flamboyantly decorated car. And he hadn't expected to see a lovely, naked woman. Her dark eyes widened as she grabbed for a fleecy towel hanging on a nearby peg. She pulled the towel to her chin, hiding the firm breasts capped with bright pink nipples and the lusciously thick dark thatch between her legs. But her expression faded from surprise to something Slocum couldn't identify.

He would have expected her to start shouting for help. Instead, she asked in a provocative voice, "Have we met?" She moved forward a little and rubbed against him. Slocum backed off, struggling to find words.

Outside, he saw the law coming for him. A search of the car would flush him for certain. Somehow, he never once considered using the woman to bargain his way to freedom.

"Name's Slocum, ma'am," he said, "and I'm in a passel of trouble right now."

"You are?" She laughed and Slocum thought of wind through the tall pines, summer days, and soft nights under starry skies. "I'm not used to finishing my bath and running into strangers."

He forced himself to tear his eyes away from her again, to judge how long before the lawmen would come to bottle him up. Not long.

"Got to go." He took a step away, smiled, and said, "It was a real pleasure seeing you, ma'am."

"Wait!" She pulled the towel around her and stepped from the tiny bathroom. "You can't blow through here, gawk at me, then run off without so much as a fare-thee-well." She turned and saw the deputies starting to search the train.

"I do have to go, unless you want to buy yourself more trouble than you can afford." He started for the rear door, but the woman grabbed his arm and held him back.

"Go and they'll catch you. What did you do?"

"More crimes than you can list," Slocum said truthfully. "Reckon the last one that's got them riled is jumping an express train from up north. Didn't have enough money for a ticket, it was coming through, and, well . . ." Slocum let his voice trail off so she could draw her own conclusion. He saw no reason to tell her about the robbery or murder charges hanging over his head.

"In here," she said, dragging him away from the rear door and toward the small bath. "Don't worry. I won't turn you over to them."

She slammed the tiny door to the bath as Slocum heard heavy pounding on the far door, the one he had used to enter.

"Hold your horses. I'm coming, I'm coming," the woman shouted. Slocum opened the door a crack and peered out. She held the towel about her in such a way that her ankles were exposed like some harlot. Slocum knew the deputies would have as hard a time as he'd had speaking to a woman in such an undressed condition. And presented with a woman obviously at home in such a fine car, they'd know they were dealing with power, also.

"Have you seen a man come through here?" the deputy in charge asked. Slocum pulled the door shut a bit more, though there was little chance any of the posse would ever look inside, with the stunning raven-haired woman standing disrobed in front of them.

"Of course I have," she said in anger. "I invited him in to my bath."

Slocum tensed, then realized she was acting in precisely the right way to get rid of the men. But one of the denser deputies spoke up. "Can we go fetch him? He's—"

"Oh!" she exclaimed, even angrier. "Who I see and what I do is my business. If you *have* to look, go on. Go on, but the general doesn't like men tracking mud into his car."

"The general? He owns this?"

"He owns the entire railroad, you ninny," the woman snapped. "Are you going to waste my time, or are you going about your business?"

The posse left, grumbling to themselves. Slocum chanced a look out the side window. No one in the posse seemed suspicious—or willing to search General Palmer's personal train without a warrant. The deputy in charge chewed them out for losing their suspect, then they began a long hike back to where they had piled the railroad ties across the Burlington Northern tracks.

Slocum turned from the window when the woman walked back to the tiny bathroom. The towel hung precariously over one perfect shoulder. The top of her left breast showed wantonly, and she didn't seem to much care.

"They've gone," she said in a low voice.

"Is this really General Palmer's personal car?" Slocum asked.

"The entire train's going to Manitou Springs. The general has a house there."

"I've heard of Glen Eyrie," Slocum allowed. He touched the brim of his Stetson and said, "I'm much obliged for the way you chased them off. They didn't want to do anything but cause me trouble."

Slocum staggered when the train began moving. He caught himself—and found the woman wrapped in his arms. The towel had fallen and neither took any note of it.

"You're dirty. If you're going to ride this train down to Manitou Springs, you ought to be clean. The general has *some* rules, after all."

"I was heading in that direction," Slocum said, wondering at his continued run of luck. The woman made no move to slip free of his circling arms.

"Then there's no reason not to accept a little hospitality. You're welcome to ride along for free, if you don't tell anyone." She turned her face up to his, and her dark eyes closed. Slocum inhaled deeply and became intoxicated by the woman's scent. Her hair was clean and sweet, and the feel of her body pressed into his was almost more than he could take. When he tried to push away, he found himself being herded into the narrow bathroom.

"It'd be a shame to waste all that heated bathwater," she said, her fingers working on his buttons. She had his shirt off before he could unbuckle his gunbelt and let it drop to the floor. Smiling wickedly, the woman dropped to her knees and began working on the tight buttons holding his canvas trousers. She persisted, and the buttons yielded, freeing Slocum from his clothing.

The woman quickly skinned him of the long underwear, then playfully shoved him backward. His legs caught the edge of the copper tub, and he tumbled in, amid a splash of water and frothy soap suds. She stood at the foot of the bathtub, smiling, her hands on her flaring, naked hips.

Slocum might have seen a more beautiful sight in his day, but he couldn't remember what it was. He told her so.

"You surely do accept what comes your way, don't you, Mr. Slocum?" Her voice was teasing, but it carried a hardness Slocum didn't understand.

"I told you my name. What's yours? I usually know the name of anyone friendly enough to share a tub."

"So?" She bent over, her breasts dangling down until they almost touched the top of the water. "What makes you think I'm going to share this tub with you?"

He grabbed her arms and pulled her in, laughing and kicking. Water sloshed over the sides and quickly drained out through the holes in the tiled floor. The train's motion caused even more to slop about, but neither noticed it. The dark-haired woman came up for air, giggling as Slocum tried to hold her in the large tub.

There wasn't any cause for him to do so. She wasn't trying to get away, but the feel of his hands sliding slickly over her soaped body excited both of them a tad more.

"Pauline," she said, tossing her head back to get the long hair away from her face. "My name's Pauline Yoakum.

Now that you know my name, how does that change anything?"

Slocum moved her about in the tub and let her settle down facing him, her legs draped over his. The woman's dark eyes widened as she felt the difference it made. She reached down in the soapy water and found the rising pillar of Slocum's manhood.

"What is this?"

"Don't tell me you've never seen one of those before," Slocum said. He shifted about so he leaned against the tub's high back, his legs bent and resting around the woman. She wiggled about and positioned herself. They both gasped when her body came down and completely surrounded his fleshy shaft.

"Oh, I know what it is," Pauline sighed. "But it's been a long time since I felt one this good." Her hips twitched from side to side, stimulating Slocum, but when she rose and slowly came back down, burying him balls-deep in her seething interior, he knew he had a fight on his hands. The pressures mounting within him made him gasp and moan. It had been a spell since he'd had a woman—and even longer since he'd found one this willing and this pretty.

Light came through a high window and caused Pauline's body to gleam. She tossed her head back and began moving with a deliberate up-and-down motion, taking him fully, then slowly sliding until he was almost free of her body. Slocum didn't have to do anything but sit in the warm water and enjoy the sensations stalking through his loins.

Reaching out, he placed his hands against those firm mounds of breast. His fingers toyed with the lust-hardened nipples until Pauline moaned constantly with pleasure. Slocum tried to lean forward and take them into his mouth, but the position was wrong and he didn't want the woman to stop her ceaseless, exciting up-and-down motion for even an instant.

His hands explored her lush body and finally came to rest cupping her muscular buttocks. This was no hothouse flower. Pauline Yoakum was a horsewoman. And horses weren't all she rode well.

She turned him inside out and every which way, and still she kept up the movement until he was at the end of his endurance.

"Can't hold back much longer," he gasped. The rocking and vibration of the train added to the thrill he got from this lovemaking. He clung to the woman as his balls tightened and tried to erupt. Iron control slipping, Slocum finally leaned back and lifted himself up out of the water as much as he could, ramming himself fully into her yielding interior.

Pauline let out a tiny shriek of pleasure as desire blasted through her. The female flesh surrounding Slocum tightened and milked him of every drop of his seed, and when he thought there wasn't anything left, Pauline did things to him to keep him going another few seconds. When he finally sagged back in the tub, he was exhausted and about as happy as he had been in weeks.

"This surely is the right way to take a bath," he said, his hands stroking her wet body.

"You haven't seen anything yet," she whispered as he leaned over. Her fingers worked under the water and found his limp length.

They reached Manitou Springs far too soon for Slocum's liking.

6

The train ground to a halt outside Manitou Springs amid a shower of bright yellow and blue sparks from the steel wheels. Slocum settled his gunbelt around his middle and then turned to his benefactor. Pauline Yoakum sat in one of the luxurious car's overstuffed chairs, her midnight eyes fixed on him intently. She had applied just a little makeup, causing her cheeks to blush and her lips to turn carmine. Some might have thought this the mark of the demimonde, but Slocum found her exciting and totally provocative. And there was no doubt the general did, too.

"How long have you been with him?" Slocum wondered about women like Pauline Yoakum. She could have any man she wanted, and there was no reason she shouldn't be with a man as rich as General Palmer. The expression on her face, though, wasn't what Slocum had expected.

She almost broke into tears. She bit her lower lip and turned from him so he couldn't see.

"Too long," she said, her voice choked with emotion. She dabbed at her eyes and turned back. If he hadn't seen the momentary lapse, he would never have known she had reacted so strongly.

"Sorry," Slocum said, meaning it.

"It's my problem," she said almost primly. "You'd better

get off here. There will be questions if anyone in the yards sees you. The men here are such gossips. I do declare. They are like a bunch of old women." She stood, took his arm, and guided him toward the rear of the car. Opening the door, she almost pushed him out. To Slocum's surprise, she followed him down the steps, carrying a small, battered carpetbag that had been sitting beside the door.

"I've never been in Manitou Springs before," Slocum said, eyeing the fancy D&RG station ahead of them along the tracks. "Is there a place to stay?" Slocum was angling to see more of Pauline, but she sidestepped him neatly.

"This is a resort town. The Saratoga of the West, they call it. You might be surprised at what you can find, if you avoid the expensive spas. Excuse me, John, but I have to go." She hurried off across the railroad tracks, never looking back. Slocum watched her go, wondering if he should follow her. He knew nothing of this town, or Colorado Springs a mile or two away, on the other side of the Garden of the Gods.

Turning from Pauline, he took in the mountains rising around him. Then he simply stared. Pikes Peak towered more than fourteen thousand feet and was still covered with snow, though it was summer. He heaved a sigh, then started walking along the tracks leading toward the peak. The yards weren't as extensive as those in Denver, but Slocum still found them complex.

If General William Jackson Palmer had a mansion here, it made sense that he wanted good rails to his home. And Slocum saw the start of tracks being laid deep into the mountains, as if the general wanted the Denver and Rio Grande to cross the Rockies here. As with so many of the D&RG lines, this was a "baby road," a narrow gauge with only three feet between rails.

"Hey, you, get out of here!" came a loud cry. Slocum saw two railroad detectives coming toward him, waving clubs in the air. They hadn't seen him get off the general's personal train. If they had, their attitude would have been different. If they had supposed he belonged there, he would have been politely greeted. On the other hand, if they thought he had been aboard illegally, they wouldn't have been walking along waving the clubs. They'd have had their guns out and shooting at him. Slocum moved along quickly, letting them herd him toward the main street.

He walked slowly along Manitou Avenue, gawking at the big city like a yokel off the farm. Slocum hadn't expected so many fine hotels. Pauline had been right saying this was a resort town catering to the rich. The smell of sulfur from the hydro spas made his nose wrinkle, but Slocum wasn't interested in soaking his body or drinking from any of the strangely named springs. Neither the Ute Chief Magnetic Springs nor the Navajo Springs appealed to him more than a shot of good whiskey.

Aware that he had only a single dollar bill in his pocket, Slocum passed several posh cafes with linen tablecloths on their tables and fine bone china services. Though his stomach complained noisily about lack of food, Slocum kept walking. He wanted to find the telegraph office and the mysterious PB.

He hiked up a steep hill to get to the Western Union office. Inside the cramped, stuffy office, a man dozed over a desk. Slocum shook his head when he saw the disarray in the office. The Fort Collins telegrapher had been neat as a pin. This office had stacks of paper everywhere, some held down by rocks or bricks, and some simply fluttered about on the floor in complete contempt for filing. To find anything in this mess would require more luck than Slocum had ever hoped for, even after spending such a delightful few hours on the train with Pauline.

Slocum coughed and woke the napping telegrapher. The man jumped, fumbled with his glasses, then peered at Slocum over the top of them. It took him a few more seconds to figure out he had a customer and respond.

"What can I do for you?" he asked in a whiskey-roughened voice. Slocum wondered if the telegrapher had been sleeping or passed out.

"I have a telegram waiting for me," Slocum said, deciding to try the same ruse he'd used in Fort Collins. Who was to say his initials weren't PB, if he knew enough about the source of the wire?

"What's the name?" Already the clerk scanned the towers of flimsy yellow sheets, as if the right one would miraculously pop out of a stack and into his hand.

"It'd be under my initials. PB. It was relayed down from Fort Collins."

"Fort Collins? I remember that one. Had a Denver origination tag on it. PB, PB, lemme see." The clerk shuffled two stacks of papers, then leaned back and looked exasperated. "You weren't supposed to come by and pick it up. It was to be delivered. I remember it all now." The clerk tapped the side of his skull. Slocum hoped nothing important had fallen out the man's ear.

"Seeing as how you remember the wire, could you just tell me what it said?"

"Can't do that, even if I did remember exactly. And I don't remember exactly. It was a curious message, that I remember. A string of numbers. Didn't make sense."

"That's what I need," Slocum said, wondering if he should concoct a new lie to explain away the numbers. He knew the railroad, that the gold was in a secret compartment in a freight car, and all he wanted now was a serial number for the boxcar. "Just the first couple numbers would help me out a great deal."

"So many wires come through. Not like the old days. Can't remember all the traffic firsthand. Truly, I can't." The man's aggravation turned to reminiscence, and Slocum wanted to skedaddle before he got fired up with telling how it used to be in the good old days.

"I'm heading on back to Denver in a few hours," Slocum said, not knowing when the next train left. "I'd appreciate it if you could tell me where the telegram ended up."

"Why, it was sent over to the Barker House, with the rest of the 'grams for Ruxton Park and Lake House. You might have missed it by now, but maybe not. Depends on how often they send a boy down to pick up mail and supplies."

"It'll be at the Barker House?" Slocum asked, not quite daring to repeat what he'd heard. He had no idea where any of these places were, but the Lake House sounded like something stuck up on the mountainside toward Pikes Peak.

"Reckon so." The clerk grabbed at sheets flying about the office and tried to weigh them down with his elbow as he reached for a pencil. The telegraph began clattering as he tried to control the papers and record the incoming message. Slocum used this opportunity to slip out of the office and look around from his vantage point atop the hill.

The Barker House had to be one of the fancy hotels scattered around town. Slocum didn't think it would be hard to find. And it wasn't. The first person he asked laughed and pointed at a four-story building on Manitou Avenue, the main street through the center of town he had walked down earlier.

Slocum was hesitant about going to the front door and entering the lobby in his condition. His bath with Pauline on the train had refreshed him but had done little for his worn, dirty clothes. From the look of the place, with its one hundred twenty feet along the main street, the towers on the east and west wings, and the wide porches surrounding it, he might get tossed out of town for simply looking at it.

This was the poshest of the posh hotels, and there were more than he could count in Manitou Springs.

Slocum walked up the steep steps to the veranda, aware that people stared at him. He'd belong here one day—when he recovered the gold from the robbery. Stopping, he stared at a slip of paper posted in a glass case beside the main door. It took a few seconds of puzzling before he figured it out.

At eight-thirty, an orchestra would begin playing no fewer than sixteen dances, ranging from the waltz to the Dan Tucker and the Virginia Reel. Slocum checked his watch and saw that the grand ball would begin shortly. He hoped this would distract enough people from his mission to find the telegram Matt Burnside had sent.

"May I help you, sir?" came a polite voice. Slocum glanced over his shoulder at a liveried servant standing close behind him. "Are you interested in our grand ball and banquet? If so, proper attire is required."

Slocum wondered if the man were simply taunting him, knowing these were about the best duds Slocum was likely to have, or if some guests showed up looking like something the cat dragged in.

"I was told to come pick up a telegram," Slocum said. "The clerk at the Western Union office said it had been routed through here, on its way up to Ruxton Park."

"I see. Come this way. I'll see what the desk clerk can find for you." The man walked down the veranda, away from the main entrance. Slocum considered bulling on into the lobby, then decided against it. He'd been treated politely so far, even after the gussied-up servant had found out he wasn't one of the hotel's rich guests. They stopped at a side door.

"One moment while I see if the clerk is free." The man ducked through the door. As it opened, Slocum took a deep breath. His mouth watered at the odors pouring from the hotel's interior. The banquet the man had spoken of had to include mutton, beef, and more kinds of bread than Slocum could put a name to. The harder he sniffed, the more he separated out individual favorites and savored their odors. A man could explode eating so many different things, he decided. And that would be his fate when he got the gold.

Slocum had a quick picture of Pauline and him sitting down to an elegant dinner at the Barker House, uniformed servants waiting on them, satisfying their every whim. And afterward, he and the lovely woman would—

"Sir, this is Mr. DeKove. He can tell you more about the telegrams." The liveried servant vanished into the growing dusk, leaving Slocum with a sour-faced man who looked more like a manager than a room clerk.

"I need the telegram addressed to—"

"They've all been picked up," snapped DeKove. "The boy from Ruxton Park picked up those destined for higher up the mountain. The others have been taken personally to our guests. Whenever will you people learn? We have a schedule to keep, and we do it. Now, be off. I must tend to the ball."

"Wait," Slocum said, grabbing the man's arm. The manager pulled away as if Slocum might be diseased. "Who picked up the telegrams?"

"Some boy. Perhaps sixteen or seventeen, blond hair, thin. The usual messenger. Andrew is his name, I believe. Now, be off. And don't let the guests catch sight of you. You are a disgrace." DeKove slammed the door behind him, but Slocum was pleased.

"Andrew," he said, making his way down a flight of stairs to the main street. "Andrew from Ruxton Park. You shouldn't be too hard to find, especially if they sent you for supplies." The boy was likely to have picked up the telegrams and other mail first, then gone to the general store so he wouldn't have to leave a wagon load of supplies while going into the Barker House.

The people strolling along the sedate streets of Manitou Springs struck Slocum as being from another world. They were obviously rich, cultured, and here for the curative mineral waters. He passed several pavilions advertising different minerals in the bath waters. Sulfur and iron made his nose twitch, but the vacationers seemed not to notice the smell.

Wandering through the streets, Slocum found a small road lined with shops of all kinds. He inquired in several after Andrew. Two didn't know him, the rest did. Slocum got the same story from all the ones who knew Andrew. He had been there shopping for the Lake House Hotel and had gone.

"Do you think he's likely to spend the night down here?"

Slocum asked a butcher. "Seems a long trip in the dark along a winding road to get back."

The butcher laughed and said, "Andrew's probably made his excuses already. He's sweet on a maid over at the Barker House. I told him I wouldn't have the side of bacon and the rest he wanted till tomorrow morning, which suits him just fine."

"So he'll be back here when you open?"

"I'm working by six," the butcher said. "Andrew might take longer because it'll be a long night for him, if you catch my meaning."

Slocum thanked the butcher and stepped back into the street, his eyes going to the lofty structure of the Barker House. If he had simply bided his time, Andrew would have returned. But now Slocum knew where to find the delivery boy. How many maids could the Barker House have, even as grand as it was?

"In the morning," Slocum muttered as he thought on the matter, "or now." He could find a place to sleep but decided against it. He had lost his gear back in Denver, and Manitou Springs was high up in the mountains. It might be summer, but the nights would get mighty cold, and with only a dollar in his pocket, he wasn't likely to find any decent place to sleep in a resort town.

"Andrew, you're going to make me rich tonight," Slocum vowed. He started for the resort hotel, intent on getting the telegram before it vanished up the slopes of Pikes Peak.

He trooped back to the hotel, this time avoiding the broad veranda where several couples now danced. The strains of music from the ballroom drifted out on the cool night air. Slocum went to the servants entrance in the rear and slipped inside, looking around. He saw a small desk covered with papers that might belong to whoever ran the kitchen. Not sure what he sought, Slocum began pawing through the papers.

"What are you doing?" A military click of boot heels sounded on the floor behind him. He turned to face an irate man weighing at least three hundred pounds. As big around as he was tall, the man threatened to pop out of his formal dress tuxedo.

"Who are you?" Slocum asked.

"I am the concierge, and I am not hiring menials. In any case, you should come around in the morning, not during the gala."

The man struggled with his thin waxed mustache, which kept fraying at the ends.

"I'm looking for Andrew. I've got an important message for him. From Lake House." Slocum made a vague gesture in the direction of Pikes Peak.

"Oh, him." The concierge managed to combine contempt and envy in a mere two words. "I assume he is with Miss Fairleigh."

"In her room?"

"I should say not! I would dismiss her at the merest hint of impropriety!" The concierge settled his immense bulk in the chair and searched the papers for whatever he had come to find. He looked up at Slocum. "They enjoy a late walk toward Navajo Springs. It is the artesian well feeding this hotel's spas."

Slocum didn't bother thanking the man. He quickly went outside and sniffed the wind. The strongest sulfur odor came from along a well-tended, rock-lined path leading higher up the hill. Slocum set off, intent on finding Andrew and his Miss Fairleigh before they got too involved with each other.

Laughter from small houses set off the path told Slocum that the Barker House had many hydro spas, and the boy he sought might be in any of them. Slocum kept walking, thinking that if he were a youngster with a first love, farther away would be better—as far as possible from the hotel's guests.

He paused as he tramped along the steep path, then turned and looked behind him. The sensation of someone quite near burned in him now. He stepped off the path and into deep shadows for a few minutes, hoping to catch sight of anyone trailing him. The bright, shrill laughter and loud splashing came from several small pavilions, but he saw no one else on the path.

Slocum had stayed alive by listening to his inner voice, and it told him now that he was not alone. Doubling back on the path availed him little, other than a quick glimpse into one spa. A half-naked woman frolicked with two men, both buck naked. Slocum shook his head. The rich weren't much different from other folks, except that they had more money.

He pulled himself away from the erotic spectacle going on inside the spa and kept walking. Fifteen minutes of hiking brought him almost to the top of the mountain. Soft voices came drifting down to him on the gentle night breeze.

" . . . do so love you, Andrew," a girl said.

"When can we get married?"

Slocum didn't cotton much to interrupting, but the Siren's call of a hundred pounds of gold was stronger even than young love. He coughed and got the couple's attention.

"Who are you?" demanded Andrew. The boy shot to his feet and tried to look tough. He was almost as tall as Slocum, but skinnier than a rail. He had flaming red hair and freckles so large they appeared to be liver spots.

"Don't want to disturb you longer than necessary. I was supposed to get a telegram, but you'd accidentally picked it up. It's taken me a while to track you down."

"I don't understand." Andrew moved to block Slocum's view of the hotel maid.

"You picked up the telegrams bound for the Lake House Hotel. You accidentally got mine. I want it because it's the last message from someone I dearly love." Slocum thought this touch might spur the young lover faster than anything else to hand over the telegram.

"I've already sent the telegrams uphill, mister," Andrew

said. "I just waited around for some supplies that won't be ready until tomorrow morning."

"Who took the telegrams?"

Andrew's mouth opened, but no words formed. The bullet hit him square in the face, and he slumped backward, into his girlfriend's arms. Slocum had seen enough dead men in his day to know that Andrew would never tell him who had taken the telegrams.

A second shot killed the maid, and the third came winging after John Slocum.

7

The breath of hot lead caressed Slocum's ear and left behind a whiff of pain that moved him faster than the mere worry of being shot ever could. He plunged forward into the darkness, tripped over Andrew's outstretched legs, and slammed hard to the rocky ground. More bullets sought him. Slocum rolled to one side, stopped, and quickly rolled to the other. This sudden movement kept him from taking a round smack-dab in the gut. A tiny puff of dirt and rock kicked up where he might have been if he hadn't changed directions when he did.

Fumbling under him, he drew his Colt Navy and sat up, looking for the telltale tongue of orange flame licking the darkness. He didn't move a muscle, hoping to lure the hidden gunman out. Slocum saw nothing and heard nothing, save for the ringing in his ears from the gunshots.

Cautiously getting to his feet, he found a large boulder and made his way around it, hoping to come up on the back-shooter's blind side. It was a good plan, but he found no trace of the mysterious gunman. Slocum waited another minute, straining hard to hear any sound.

He jerked to the left barely in time to save himself from being slugged on the head with a large rock thrown from above him. Somehow the sidewinder trying to plant Slocum in a shallow grave had gotten above him with all the skill of a stalking Apache.

Slocum swung his six-shooter up and fired twice, to keep the man above him moving and off balance. This time Slocum heard the grating of boots against sandstone and knew where his assailant had gone. Unfortunately for Slocum, there wasn't time enough to use this faint telltale sound to get into the right position for protecting himself. Another shot rang out, almost ending Slocum's life.

He crouched down and heard the sound of a gun being reloaded. Slocum didn't know who was shooting at him or why. It was hard to believe the deputy who had tracked him to Fort Collins could have arrived in Manitou Springs this fast. Slocum considered his tracks obscured from Fort Collins, thanks to Pauline's kind offer to ride in the general's personal rail car.

Who was shooting at him?

Slocum knew he couldn't make a fight of it. He didn't have enough ammunition, and explaining two dead bodies to the law was out of the question. He slid down the side of the mountain, cutting himself on sharp stone and even pricklier vegetation. But he didn't escape. He saw a dark outline above and the foot-long tongue of hungry flame as the back-shooter fired on him again. Slocum wiggled and twisted and dodged the best he could as he slid down the slope, but he knew he'd be a goner if he didn't think fast.

He came to the edge of a ten-foot drop and succeeded in grabbing a rocky outcropping. Just below was the roof of a hydro spa. Slocum hung for a second, dropped, rolled a few feet, then dropped again, this time landing hard on the ground beside the entrance. The odor of sulfur almost overpowered him. The hot mineral waters were supposed to be the best restorative available for whatever ailed a body, and drinking them did even more to maintain or improve health. Slocum hoped that that was true as he ducked inside.

He heard faint moans and searched the ponds under the roof, finding a naked man in one of the baths. Beside the bath were two champagne bottles. If the man had emptied them by himself, he was lucky not to be dead. Slocum pulled the man's pudgy, pasty face up, and his eyelids twitched and opened.

"Who're you? My good buddy. Gimme more," the man said as he slipped back into unconsciousness. Slocum made certain he wouldn't drown, then grabbed the man's clothes. He held them up and decided the fit would be good enough. He was a couple inches taller, but the man in the pond was heavier set. Slocum quickly stripped off his grimy rags and got into the man's clothes.

He bundled up his gunbelt and hid it under a fluffy white towel before leaving. He tapped down the man's sporty bowler, but the man's head was too small, causing the hat to perch atop Slocum's like a crow on a fence. Slocum tossed the hat away and shoved his own mangled Stetson under his arm before leaving the spa. If whoever had ambushed him earlier saw him walking along, Slocum hoped the gunman would think he was only a guest at the Barker House out for a night's soak in the mineral baths.

He tried not to break into a run when he heard voices behind him. He didn't know if the ambusher worked alone or had a partner. So far, the gunman had played it cagey and hadn't made any mistakes. Slocum doubted the killer would now. He turned and looked behind. His heart leapt when he saw three people swaddled like ghosts in the white towels furnished by the Barker House. More guests had partaken of the restorative mineral spas and now returned to the hotel.

"Did you enjoy the bath?" came a woman's voice, too shrill and grating to be endured. Slocum tried to put her off, but she rushed up and took his arm.

She wore too much makeup and was more than a little drunk. But for all the liquor in her, her grip was strong. She clung to his arm like a cougar with a lamb.

"Refreshing," Slocum said. He looked behind the small group, up the slope, and thought he saw a shadow move.

Not sure, he turned and put his arm around the woman. "Let's return to the hotel," he suggested. With the others around him, getting shot in the back was less likely.

"A splendid idea. We can raid their kitchen. The cook has some of the most delightful *pommes croquettes*. But you must know that. They were served at dinner."

Slocum didn't have any idea what the food the inebriated woman had mentioned might be, so he only nodded as he steered her down the path, hoping to reach the relative safety of the hotel before the gunman behind him got into position for a better shot.

"Not so fast, Adeline," complained one of the two women behind them. "We can't keep up with you and your gentleman friend."

Slocum saw that the other two women were close to falling-down drunk. One waved a champagne bottle about, and the other tried repeatedly to grab it, missing each time.

"We haven't been introduced, have we?" asked the woman on his arm. "You are such a strong fellow. I'm Adeline Grimsby."

"Pleased to meet you, and the other ladies," Slocum said, trying not to pin a name on himself.

"My husband's Hector Grimsby, the hardware store magnate. Owns who knows how many stores throughout Colorado."

"Owns two over in Cripple Creek, another in Pueblo and six in Denver. Filthy rich, filthy," muttered the woman who had yet to grab the champagne bottle. From her tone, Slocum knew there was more than a little animosity over the difference in the women's bank accounts. The bottle of wine they fought over probably cost more than the single greenback in Slocum's pocket.

At the thought, Slocum groaned. He had left the bill tucked in his shirt pocket—and the shirt had been discarded back at the hydro spa. He was penniless, unless the bather had a few dollars in his pockets. Slocum would have hunted for any spare change, but Adeline Grimsby clung too tenaciously to his arm. The circulation started to die.

"There's the hotel," Slocum said, hoping this would shake her loose. "Let's go to our rooms, change, and—"

"Oh, no," Adeline Grimsby said, moving even closer. Slocum felt her flaring hip pressing into his thigh. "That would be no fun at all. Let's go to your room and see what happens."

Slocum glanced behind at the other two women. They tittered and covered their mouths with their hands, exchanging whispered comments. From the way their drunken eyes sparkled, though, Slocum knew if Adeline Grimsby hadn't been the one making the proposition, either or both of them would have.

"That's not a good idea," Slocum said, trying to choose his words carefully. He didn't want to offend them. If the woman was rich, she was used to getting her way. Slocum didn't want a vendetta sworn on him by a rejected lover. He had problems enough brewing elsewhere. Two people lay dead on the mountain trail, and he would have been the third if he hadn't moved fast enough.

"Oh, you're married. That's no problem for me if you are discreet," Adeline Grimsby said, tilting her head back and puckering her lips. "Kiss me and I'll let you go."

The brunette woman wasn't bad looking. Slocum had seen worse in his day, but he couldn't keep the comparison with Pauline Yoakum from entering his thoughts. Pauline was a beauty, truly gorgeous, vivacious and alive. She had wit and intelligence and all the things that sparked Slocum's interest most.

The best he could say about Adeline Grimsby was that she was willing. The woman was drunk, she wore too much makeup, and her nose was her most prominent feature.

"Kiss me or I'll raise a ruckus," she warned. Her lips curled back, and her tongue darted out suggestively.

"We wouldn't want that, would we?" Slocum kissed her

lightly on the lips, but the woman wasn't satisfied. She clutched him with a ferocious passion that almost took his breath away. Her tongue forced its way into his mouth and boldly challenged his to a wrestling match. Slocum managed to pry her loose and step back, holding her at arm's length.

"You're more than I can handle," he said earnestly. "Doesn't your husband object to you acting like this?"

"Hector?" she scoffed. "He's probably in some poker game. That's all he ever does. Work and gamble, work and gamble. He hardly knows I exist. I get so lonely. A young, beautiful woman's got needs." She pulled Slocum back to her. "And a big, handsome buck like you can give me what I want most."

She kissed him again, but this time Slocum didn't respond. He backed off, not wanting to get involved further with her.

"I'm a bit woozy from the mineral baths," he lied. "I need to change clothes. We can meet, all four of us, in the bar. For a drink."

"The bar closed hours ago," Adeline said, "but I have a few bottles of champagne in my room. We can share it— and the bed."

They slowly climbed the steep steps leading to the Barker House's main doors. Slocum turned on the top tread and tried to catch any hint of someone on his trail. Shadows danced in the flickering light from dozens of gaslights along the hotel veranda. He was all too aware that he presented any sharpshooter a perfect target, outlined against the bright lights. He moved closer to the main doors, keeping Adeline Grimsby between him and any back-shooter.

Slocum wasn't proud of using the woman as a shield, but he had to stay alive if he wanted to retrieve the gold Burnside had hidden. And his curiosity was beginning to get the better of him. Who stalked him through the Barker House spas?

"What quaint clothing," Adeline Grimsby said, running

her fingers along his lapels. For the first time Slocum got a good look at the clothes he had stolen.

He was decked out like a riverboat dandy. The expensive red silk cravat, with a big diamond stickpin, hung around his neck and presented stark contrast to the boiled white shirt. The jacket was tight across the shoulders, causing seams to creak in protest as he moved, but the pants were adequate. What Slocum lacked in girth he needed in length. Any tailor worth his salt would have sneered at the poor fit, but Adeline Grimsby never noticed.

Nor did she notice the six-shooter he clutched under the white towel draped over his right arm.

"You're so jumpy. Relax," she urged. "My husband does not care what I do. This is a vacation, this is a resort. Enjoy!"

She tried to kiss him again. A bull-throated roar echoed through the lobby and froze Slocum in his tracks. He saw a huge man bolt like a stuck pig, rushing from a card room toward Slocum and the woman. The man's sausage-like fingers opened and closed, seeking something to strangle. From the way he stumbled as he came, Slocum realized the man was drunker than a lord.

He also knew that this was Hector Grimsby, the hardware magnate husband who didn't care what his wife did on her vacation—or so said Adeline Grimsby.

"Get your filthy hands off her, you philanderer!" shouted Grimsby. He thundered past the two women who had been with his wife, pushing them out of the way, and came at Slocum.

Slocum had his Colt Navy in his hand, but he wasn't going to shoot an unarmed man. He had seen others who didn't much care, but he did. Instead of shooting, he side-stepped and let Grimsby stumble past. He thrust out a foot and sent the man belly flopping through the door and onto the veranda.

By now, the desk clerk had rushed around and hastened to Grimsby's aid.

"Oh, sir, are you hurt?"

"Get your hands off me, you drone." Grimsby shoved the clerk away. "I want your ears nailed on my shed!" Grimsby fought to get to his feet, but Slocum simply stood his ground, waiting for what would happen. As the hardware store owner grabbed for him, Slocum turned to one side and tugged a little on Adeline Grimsby's arm.

Husband and wife went down in a pile on the floor, struggling to get to their feet.

"You're a dead man. You can't molest my little Adeline and expect to get away with it." Grimsby struggled to grab Slocum, but he was easily turned aside because of his drunken state.

"Bad night at cards," Slocum said to the desk clerk, as he continued to push Grimsby just enough to keep the man off balance. "He gets this way. There's no need to call the authorities."

"Sir, we take care of our guests!" the clerk said huffily. "We would never summon the law for such an affront."

"Mr. Grimsby needs help. Big losses at cards tonight, his drinking is getting worse, other problems worry at him." Slocum looked at Adeline Grimsby and saw she might be the corpulent man's biggest difficulty. Her eyes glowed as she saw her man trying to defend what must have been tarnished honor.

"Get him out of the hotel until he cools off," the clerk said. "Do it and the management will look quite favorably upon you."

"I understand," Slocum said, grabbing Grimsby's arm as the man flailed at him. They staggered back, and suddenly Slocum found the tables turned. Grimsby's weight pinned him against the wall.

"I challenge you to a duel for besmirching my wife's reputation. I challenge you to a duel to the death, you yellow-bellied coward!" Grimsby shook Slocum so hard his teeth rattled. Slocum pushed the man away and tried to regain his senses. He had been shot at, gone without sleep, had too little to eat, and been thwarted at every turn in regaining the stolen gold.

He was at the end of his rope.

"Nobody calls me a coward," he said. His fingers tightened around the butt of his Colt Navy, his trigger finger finding just the right spot to loose a round into this fat fool's gut.

"A duel, an affair of honor," squealed Adeline Grimsby. "How brave of you, Hector!"

Slocum relaxed as the intoxicated woman interposed herself between him and Hector Grimsby. Then Slocum saw real trouble brewing. He would have preferred to deal with the murdering back-shooter prowling around the mineral springs. Six men came from the card room to see what the fuss was.

"A duel," cried one. "Splendid. Out back, on the croquet court. It is a perfect time of night for it."

Slocum found himself being pushed along by four men, while two others and Adeline Grimsby herded her husband. The woman seemed more enthralled with the idea that her husband would die than with any defense of her honor. They went along the side of the Barker House and out to a grassy area behind the kitchens. Slocum tried to get free but found that it was like fighting a dust devil. No matter where he turned, he found himself being battered and tormented.

"There," one man said with some glee. "Back-to-back. Ten paces, turn, and fire."

Slocum's towel was yanked from his hand. With the towel went his trusty six-gun. A small two-shot derringer with ivory grips was thrust into his hand. Somehow he found himself back-to-back with a shaking Hector Grimsby. He could only guess that the hardware store owner was similarly armed.

"Fifty dollars on Hector," spoke up one onlooker.

"A hundred on the other gentleman. He has the look of a true duelist. See the steely glint in his eye?"

Slocum didn't feel steely at the moment, but he knew he could kill Hector Grimsby with no effort at all. The man was drunk and unsteady on his feet, furious at seeing another man cuckolding him, and goaded past fury by his card-playing friends. If Grimsby could even find his target, it would be a miracle.

"One!" cried an onlooker.

And Slocum took a pace, knowing he was going to be in a stew pot of trouble if he fired. And he'd be dead if he didn't.

"Two!"

Slocum took another step, then whirled about before the count of three, leveling his derringer. He knew what he had to do.

8

Slocum closed the distance with two long steps, reached out, and grabbed Hector Grimsby's collar, swinging the man about. With his other hand he knocked away the derringer. The man was so drunk he hardly knew what had happened.

"What're you doing?" came the outraged demand from an onlooker who had bet heavily on Slocum. "This is an affair of honor. You're violating—"

"I'm violating nothing," snapped Slocum. "I'm not going to kill a man who can hardly stand up."

"How dare you say that?" Grimsby tried to bring the derringer around and drill Slocum in the belly. Slocum knocked the small two-shot pistol aside again. It discharged with a report that echoed down the valley.

"This is no duel, it's a murder," Slocum said. He took aim and blew the hat off the man who had goaded Grimsby to the duel. The second barrel begged to be fired a few inches lower, but Slocum hung back. He'd made his point.

"This is a matter of honor," complained someone else, irate at being cheated of a moment's diversion at someone else's expense. Slocum tried to figure out if Grimsby had been a winner or loser at the poker game, or if these men were simply rich and bored with life. He had seen too many men die to take any pleasure in it.

"Then we should fight like men," Slocum said.

"What are you saying? Are you impugning my manhood?" The hardware magnate puffed himself up, giving Slocum an even bigger target. Slocum knew what he wanted to do to Grimsby, and that course seemed downright appropriate.

"A fight," Slocum said, correctly judging the mood of the crowd and their desire to see blood. "A fistfight. Bare knuckles, here and now." He tucked the derringer into a vest pocket, worried about what had happened to his Colt Navy. He saw the towel some distance away but wasn't sure his sidearm was still wrapped in it.

"Fisticuffs! Splendid!" General approval ran through the crowd, but one man protested.

"There ought to be some spice to the fight. Neither of these men is John L. Sullivan. We are not mere brawlers here. Where is the honor if they simply fall down?"

"What do you suggest?" asked Slocum, warily watching Grimsby. The man seemed drunker now than before, and behind him stood his wife. Adeline Grimsby basked in the attention this generated. And Slocum didn't like the way the woman eyed him. He had seen vultures with less hunger in their eyes.

"The roof. The roof of the hotel. There is a ledge. Fight on the ledge!" Someone suggested.

This met with great approval. Slocum looked up four stories to the edge of the Barker House's roof and shuddered. A fall from any point along the verge would mean death. He had no fear of heights or meeting Grimsby in a fight, but he didn't want to kill the man. If he had intended to finish him off, Slocum would have simply turned and fired a bullet into the man's head. He feared this was going to blossom into a battle that would attract the town marshal.

A local lawman might start wondering about Slocum—or remember a wanted poster—and contact Denver. If that happened, all hell would be out for lunch, and Slocum would have no chance ever to find out who PB was and get the last clue needed to retrieve the gold. He would find himself dodging the law all the way from here to the Mexican border.

"I'm game," Grimsby said, glaring at Slocum and turning to say something to his wife. Slocum couldn't hear what Adeline Grimsby retorted, but a flush came to her cheeks and she stamped her foot angrily. Her coterie of female friends clustered around her, chattering like magpies.

Slocum found himself carried along by the crowd. As he was hustled along, he stooped and scooped up his Colt Navy and the towel wrapped around it. He felt better with it, even if his position was turning more precarious by the moment. He had little chance to appreciate the luxury of the hotel as the men pushed and shoved him to the stairs. Slocum stopped fighting and cooperated, to the men's obvious delight. They were no better than vultures circling, waiting for dinner to die in the middle of the desert.

"How much is bet on me?" Slocum asked one man.

"Odds are three to one. Want to take some of the action?"

Slocum shook his head. He had no money to bet and would either have his head busted open when he fell off the roof or find himself in jail for killing the hardware salesman. Grimsby stripped off his shirt and bellowed like a bull.

Slocum kept from laughing at the sight. Grimsby was a big man, but it was all bouncing mounds of fat. Still, Slocum didn't underestimate him. The man must have put in long hours loading hardware at one time to reach his current exalted position as owner of a chain of stores. There would be muscles behind the huge fists that were now balled and shaking in Slocum's direction.

"Come on, you philanderer!" shouted Grimsby. He wobbled slightly on the edge of the roof. "Come and get your comeuppance!"

Slocum stepped out, balancing carefully on the edge of the roof. The sloping shingles on his left slanted up steeply. To his right was a sheer four-story drop. He put his left foot forward and brought up his fists, estimating distances carefully. Slocum was almost knocked off the roof by Grimsby's mad rush forward, arms flailing.

Slocum blocked one punch and took another on his upper arm. He kept his head down, trying to judge Grimsby's skill. Slocum found it impossible. Grimsby showed no ability at all. When he realized this, Slocum kept his head down and stepped forward. He jabbed, caught Grimsby in the gut, and then followed with two quick rights to the man's face.

Grimsby staggered and would have fallen if Slocum hadn't grabbed his opponent's arm and steadied him. This produced a loud jeer from the onlookers. Slocum saw every window along the roof filled with faces. Dozens watched the fight.

"Finish him, finish him off!" came the cry. Slocum wasn't sure if they meant him or Grimsby. Not that it mattered to any of the spectators.

Grimsby recovered and came back at him with his windmill punches. Slocum took another heavy blow on the shoulder that staggered him. He dropped to one knee, staring forty feet to the ground. Grimsby tried to use his weight to crush Slocum, to throw him from the hotel roof. Slocum grunted and stood, picking the man up and shoving him so hard that he staggered.

Grimsby fell heavily while Slocum watched. He ignored the shouts for him to finish the fight. His shoulder ached from the pounding he had taken, and his fists were throbbing with dull pain. He flexed his fingers, then balled them again when he saw Grimsby getting back to his feet.

"Give it up," Slocum said to the hardware salesman. "You can't win."

"You were fooling around with Adeline," Grimsby grated as he started back for Slocum. "This is going to be the last time! I'll show her what I do to her fancy men!"

Grimsby's clumsy attack presented Slocum with his best

chance to end the fight. The man's double chin quivered as Slocum caught him squarely with an uppercut that snapped Grimsby's head back. A second punch to the belly doubled Grimsby up, and a final uppercut knocked him from the roof. Slocum was off balance and couldn't grab him. He watched the man twist in the air, out like a light.

"The trees!" someone laughed. "He landed in a tree. He's sleeping like a hibernating bear!"

Slocum recovered and gripped the edge of the roof. Grimsby hung like a corpulent sheet over a limb ten feet away. The faint moans from the man told Slocum he was unhurt. When he came to, he might be loaded to the muzzle with rage, but he would be alive.

"Congratulations!" Slocum half turned and found himself surrounded by the women who had accompanied Adeline Grimsby. One woman kissed him, and another tried. Slocum had to catch her to keep the woman from falling off the roof.

"You're so strong. One punch. You knocked him out with a single punch."

Slocum tried to correct that and found it impossible. Someone shoved a bottle of champagne into his hands. He drank and found his mouth otherwise occupied by still another woman intent on lionizing him for his victory over Grimsby.

He forced his way off the roof and into an upper hallway in the hotel. He pressed against a wall to shut off the circle of adoring fans around him. But Slocum was startled when the man who had instigated the fight shoved a sheaf of greenbacks at him.

"Your cut. If you ever want to fight professionally, look me up. Oliver Walcott. Here's my card."

"Oh, you hero, you were so brave. You defended my honor!" Adeline Grimsby elbowed aside the other women and got to the front. Her friends tittered and slowly vanished, going down the stairs into the main part of the hotel. Only Slocum and the woman were left in the upper hallway, and he felt increasingly uneasy with her.

"You'd better be seeing to your husband, Mrs. Grimsby," Slocum said, edging toward the stairs. Adeline Grimsby followed like a bloodhound.

"My husband is out for hours. Even if he recovers, how are we going to get him out of the tree until he sobers up?" She grabbed his arm and pulled closer, rubbing against him like a cat. She stopped short of purring. "You're so different from Hector. You're strong and brave. And you must be different from him in other ways." Her hand pressed into Slocum's crotch.

He pushed away from her, uneasily looking around. He couldn't punch her out as he had done her husband. Slocum tried a different tactic.

"I'll buy you a drink."

"The bar's not open," she said. "Why not come to my room? There is a bottle of champagne just waiting to be opened."

Slocum had gone down two flights of stairs and was trying to turn at the landing to reach a lower level when he heard gruff voices from below.

"Don't much care what you do to preserve the reputation of your guests, Mr. DeKove. We got to keep the peace, and there's been quite a ruckus up there on your roof. The guests in a couple other hotels complained about it."

"Really, Marshal, this is petty jealousy from other establishments. Nothing untoward has happened. My staff can attend to any problem."

"You got a half-naked man dangling three stories up in a tree, DeKove," snapped the lawman. "Let's get him down and see what he has to say for himself."

"Perhaps we can—"

Slocum didn't stick around to hear the rest of the manager's protests. He held out his arm to Adeline Grimsby and said, "That champagne sounds like what I need." He heard the marshal and his deputy starting up the steps.

"My room is just down the hall," she said eagerly, almost

dragging Slocum along. He didn't tarry, wanting as he did to get out of sight as fast as possible, no matter the price he might have to pay. Adeline Grimsby shoved him into a room and slammed the door behind him just as the marshal came into the hall.

Slocum let the woman lock the door. He stood and stared at the room. He had expected luxury but nothing like this. What caught his eye and held it was the four-poster bed dominating the center of the room. Adeline Grimsby bounced on it, patting the spot beside her suggestively.

"Do come and join me. There are no comfortable chairs in this room. You would think for twenty dollars a night they would have a . . . love seat." Adeline Grimsby batted her eyelashes at him in what she thought was a seductive gesture.

"Where's the champagne?" Slocum asked. He saw it in a silver serving bucket and went to pop the cork. He turned to ask where the glasses were, thinking a glass or two and he would be on his way. Seeing a naked Adeline Grimsby lounging on the bed in what she must have thought was a seductive pose froze Slocum.

"We don't need glasses," she said. "Pour some right here. And lick it off." She stroked her belly and ran her hands up to her conical breasts, cupping them with both hands.

"Your husband will be back anytime. I don't want to—"

"He has his own room. He always insists on it. Now I understand how wonderful this arrangement can be." She moved her legs so that Slocum caught sight of the chestnut thatch between her thighs. Adeline Grimsby reached out for him.

Slocum started for her, taking a few seconds to dribble champagne over her body. Adeline moaned softly and leaned back on the soft bed, her eyes closed and lips pursed. Slocum bent over and kissed her lightly. This wasn't enough for the woman. She grabbed him and pulled him down hard.

Slocum's body crushed Adeline Grimsby's. The woman kissed him hard and wasn't going to let him go free. She had found a hero and wanted him to share her bed. Slocum's hands drifted to cup the woman's breasts, kneading gently, teasing, tormenting, building her passion. He had somehow hoped this would be enough to satisfy her.

It only whetted her appetite.

"Take me, my strong buck. Take me hard!" She tried to work off the pants Slocum had stolen.

"Wait," he said, backing off. "I need to go to my room for a moment."

"What?"

Slocum darted for the door and opened it. He closed it almost as fast. Two deputies stood just down the corridor, arms crossed and looking as if they were staked out for the night. Slocum closed the door and turned, bumping into Adeline Grimsby.

She worked to get his fly open, her fingers fumbling past the buttons to find his manhood. Slocum groaned as her lips fastened on the tip of his organ. He tried to pirouette but found that this only shoved his slowly hardening length deeper into the woman's mouth. His knees turned weak and wobbly, reminding Slocum that he had been through hell in the past forty-eight hours.

And there had been a touch of heaven, too. He couldn't forget Pauline Yoakum, especially now that Adeline was vying for that memory. Slocum should have fought harder to get away, but his legs wouldn't move.

"Don't," Slocum said, not sure if he really meant it. He reached down and put his hands on Adeline Grimsby's head. She moved back and forth now, her lips curled firmly around him. The woman started a gentle suction that caused Slocum to harden quickly.

"So long, so hard, my hero," she mumbled around the thick plug in her mouth. Slocum felt her hot breath gusting across his groin and knew he wasn't going to fight her off. She wasn't Pauline, but Adeline presented a better alternative than walking into the open arms of the lawmen outside.

"Here," Slocum said, fumbling around so that he could pour champagne down the front of his pants. The wine crossed the woman's lips. She turned her face up, a large smile on her face. Slocum poured more champagne, and Adeline Grimsby drank greedily. And she returned to his groin greedily—sucking, licking, and using her tongue in ways that kept Slocum weak in both knees and determination.

"You're tasty," she cooed, her hands stroking up and down the backs of Slocum's legs. She squeezed his ass, fingers like steel. Slocum turned slightly, and the woman followed, as if she were glued to him. The lewd sounds coming from her lips caused Slocum to get even harder. He didn't want to be here with her, but he couldn't get away. Not now, not like this.

"More wine?" he asked.

"Why not? It'll make our midnight repast all the more . . . delectable," Adeline Grimsby said. She drank deeply. Slocum sat on the floor next to her and kissed her, his hands stroking along the line of her jaw and tangling in the hair swaying loosely behind her head. He let her finish the champagne and escaped her for a moment to get more.

He found a second bottle on the floor, warm and unappetizing. But Slocum popped the cork and let Adeline suck up the foam. She immediately went back to sucking on something warmer and harder, much to Slocum's confusion. He enjoyed the attention even as he wanted to get away.

"To the bed," he said, handing her the second bottle of wine. Adeline Grimsby drank as he picked her up and deposited her on the bed. She giggled and reached out to him. He took a drink from the bottle and handed it back to her. As she drank another time, he stroked along the woman's naked body, tweaking both blood-engorged nipples and moving even lower.

Slocum paused when Adeline Grimsby mumbled something he didn't quite understand, then rolled onto her side, snoring loudly. The wine had finally taken its toll on the woman.

Slocum slipped from the bed, aware of his aroused condition. He heaved a sigh, knowing that getting cold feet when it came to bedding another man's wife was smart. Let Adeline Grimsby think what she wanted. Not that much had happened.

She might brag to Hector Grimsby about her conquest, but Slocum wasn't going to be around long enough to find out. He got his fly buttoned, went to the window, and looked out.

The marshal and a deputy struggled to get Hector Grimsby from the tree. Slocum went back to the door leading into the corridor and peered out in time to hear the marshal bellowing for help. The two lawmen grumbled but left their post to help.

Slocum slipped out and hurried down the stairs, intent once more on getting back the gold he and his partners had stolen fair and square.

9

Slocum struggled to keep the towel around his shoulders to ward off some of the cold. It might be getting near summer, but at this altitude in the Rockies it got damned cold at night. Slocum fumbled out his watch and flipped open the cover. It would be dawn in about an hour. He could survive that long without freezing to death.

He had considered finding a mineral springs and staying there, near the bubbling warmth, but had discarded the idea when he saw how active the law was in Manitou Springs. And why shouldn't they be? It had been a busy night for them. He and Hector Grimsby had gotten into a fight that brought most of the lawmen in town to the Barker House. And Slocum worried that Andrew and his girlfriend might be found. That discovery would be like pouring boiling water down an anthill.

The marshal would be hard-pressed to arrest enough people to account for a double murder. And John Slocum would be a prime candidate.

He checked his Colt Navy and made sure the six chambers were loaded. When the stores opened in a couple hours, he would find a gunsmith and buy more ammunition. What little ammo he had was lost in his saddlebags back in the Denver rail yards. He patted a shirt pocket and knew he had the derringer given him for the duel, but it carried only one round.

His clothing was in worse shape than his weapons. The pants were stained with champagne and too short not to get him stared at if he walked along the streets. His shirt and coat were too tight by far. Just trying on the jacket caused it to rip at the shoulders. Slocum vowed to steal from someone closer to his size the next time.

The one bright spot was the wad of greenbacks he had been given after the fight. He had almost fifty dollars, which would go far in buying new clothes and ammunition. He settled back and stared down the valley toward Colorado City and the rising sun. It poked past the edges of the canyon wall and finally rose enough to give some much needed warmth.

With dawn came a stirring in Manitou Springs that bothered Slocum. The streets were being constantly patrolled by the marshal and his alert deputies. Slocum doubted they were hunting for him specifically, but there was no question that the lawmen had their noses out of joint. Slocum wasn't inclined to ask the reason.

On a backwater street, he found a store selling clothing at a decent price. Most of the shops carried fancy duds fit for a king. The tourists making their way to the hydro spas had more money than good sense, and the storekeepers played on this with the items they stocked. But Slocum was sure he had found a shop where the local citizens bought their clothing. Feeling better, he left to find a gunsmith. As he stepped into the street, he paused and then openly stared.

"Pauline!" he called, startled at seeing her. She had discarded her finery for a serviceable denim skirt and plain white cotton blouse. A checkered bandanna around her neck had the look of being used long and hard, and the battered black hat pulled down on her forehead had seen better days.

"Well, as I live and breathe," she said, smiling broadly. Slocum had seen prettier women, but he couldn't remember when or where. "I didn't expect you to stay long in town."

"I have business," Slocum said, "but it's not going the way I thought. I have to make my way up the mountain."

"To the Peak?" She pointed toward distant, snowcapped Pikes Peak.

"Not all the way," Slocum said. "Somewhere called Ruxton Park is as far as I need go."

"That's a coincidence," she said. "I work for the Lake House Hotel at Ruxton Park." Pauline saw the surprise on his face. She grinned wickedly. "You don't think I travel on the general's personal train all the time, do you?"

"I thought so," Slocum said, not understanding.

Pauline laughed in delight. "I work at the Lake House, and now and again Mr. and Mrs. Dana—they manage the hotel for Mr. Copley—send me into Denver on business." She looked around and lowered her voice to a conspiratorial whisper. "The engineer on the general's train lets me ride whenever there's no one else traveling on it. I save the money on the ticket to Denver and enjoy a bit of luxury. I feel so wicked." Pauline lowered her eyes and added, "I feel like a different person. I'm sorry if I did anything to embarrass you on the trip here."

"You're not the general's—" Slocum couldn't bring himself to say what he had thought. Pauline had done nothing to dissuade him from thinking she was General Palmer's mistress.

"How delicious! No, I'm just a poor working girl trying to save a few pennies." Pauline let out a deep sigh. "And the work gets harder all the time."

"What's wrong? Anything I can help with?" He saw the hope flare on her lovely face, then firmness come to her chin as she shook her head. "Please," Slocum insisted. "You could have put me off the train in Denver. I owe you."

"I'd say all debts were mutually paid on the trip. I was satisfied. Weren't you?" Her dark eyes locked with his green ones.

It was Slocum's turn to grin like a fool. "Not if there's a chance for another ride."

Her enjoyment seemed to fade, and her mind turned to other matters, more distant ones that Slocum didn't share.

"What can I do?" he repeated.

"Our hired hand is gone. Andrew was supposed to load a wagon with supplies and pick up a new load of passengers for the Lake House."

Slocum tensed. He knew what had happened to Andrew, but Pauline obviously still had not heard. That meant the boy's body hadn't been discovered yet.

"Does he go off like this often?"

"No, but he's been seeing a maid over at the Barker House. No one's seen her, either. I think they might have eloped. It's the kind of thing a romantic young fool like Andrew would consider." Pauline sighed again and pointed toward the wagon at the end of the street. "I can't handle a rig that large on the road going to the hotel."

"I've driven wagons before," Slocum said modestly. He had worked as a mule skinner and stagecoach driver and could handle any rig with oxen or horses in front of it.

"Would you? This would save my life. Mrs. Dana has been blaming me for everything that's been going wrong at the hotel, and none of it is my fault."

"What's not right?" Slocum asked, shifting his bundle to his left arm. He hunted a place to throw the stolen clothes without being too obvious.

"There's a new road that opened up the Fourth of July, last year. It goes up through Englemann Canyon and is more than ten miles shorter than the one from Lake House. Business is falling off at the hotel, and everyone is getting a mite nervy about it."

Slocum and Pauline walked to the wagon, which had been loaded with the meat and other goods Andrew had purchased the day before. Slocum saw that there were piles of blankets in the rear, where soft-assed tourists might ride more comfortably. He checked the wagon and saw that the axles were in good condition, as were the harness and brakes.

"Where is the team?" he asked Pauline. "I need to be sure they've been tended to before we start. I don't expect to find much water on the way up."

"There are streams. The horses can drink from Bear Creek, and this time of year there's always plenty of forage for them." Pauline chewed her lower lip and shifted nervously from foot to foot. "I do hope this will be all right with Mrs. Dana."

"Getting me to drive the tourists and supplies? I'm an old hand, and I'm not asking to get paid. I need to find someone up in Ruxton Park, so you're doing me a favor giving me a ride up."

"Whoever can you be after?" Pauline seemed to consider this aspect for the first time. "There are a few hermits up there, but most of the folks work at the hotels. Some of us are there year-round, like the crew at the Peak with the Army Signal Service. They're talking about running a telegraph line to the summit so they can get weather information."

"I'll know him when I see him," Slocum said. PB. The man with the key to enough gold to keep Slocum fat and happy for years.

"John," the dark-haired temptress started. She had a pained expression on her face. "I want to thank you for this, but—"

Slocum understood what Pauline was trying to say. What had happened on the train was past. She had acted out a fantasy of living like a rich lady who really knew important men like General Palmer. The Lake House Hotel was ahead, and the rules of the game were different now.

"I'll see to the team," he said, touching the brim of his hat.

Slocum found the stable where Andrew had left the four horses. He quickly checked their shoes and made sure their bridles were in good repair. When Pauline had rounded up her tourists, he could have the team ready in a few minutes. Slocum left the stable and stopped, staring at a well-dressed man who spoke to Pauline.

She pointed to a store down the street, and the man hurried off. Slocum went to her and asked, "Do you know him? He looks familiar, but I can't put a name to his face."

"That's one of the guests," she said. "His name's Benton."

"Benton?" That didn't ring true for Slocum. He knew the man but under another name. "Where's he heading?"

"Don't know," Pauline told him, more worried than she had been before. "I've got to see after four other guests. If we have only Mr. Benton, there'll be hell to pay. The other hotels have been luring our guests away. Mr. Dana will be fit to be tied if the Halfway House is making a better offer on getting to the Peak. There is a cog railroad going in that will draw tourists, and . . ." Pauline rushed off in a dither, muttering to herself. Slocum didn't like seeing her this agitated. Still, no matter how excited she got, she had to be one of the most beautiful women in Colorado.

Slocum turned his attention from Pauline Yoakum to her tourist. Benton vanished into a general store a ways down Canon Street. On impulse, Slocum walked down the boardwalk and stopped in front of the large plate glass window. He peered inside and saw Benton walking up one aisle and down another. The clerk watched Benton like a hawk, but neither said a word.

Again Slocum felt the twinges of memory, and once more the memory refused to return.

When a second customer entered the store, the clerk turned to greet the woman. Slocum saw Benton move like a striking snake, his hands going out to ladle in a card of needles, thread, and a thin-bladed knife from a display counter. Slocum blinked, and Benton sauntered from the store as if nothing had happened. If Slocum hadn't been so intent on the man, he might have missed the theft.

All told, Benton couldn't have taken more than a few dollars' worth of goods. But he had gone into the store with the intent of stealing. Slocum read it in the man's face, and this wasn't a theft done because Benton needed the goods. He had swiped the thread and needles simply for the thrill of pilfering.

"Benton," Slocum muttered, watching the man walk off as if he didn't have a care in the world. The name was close but not right. Slocum followed at a distance, watching as the would-be tourist stole minor items from a half dozen other stores.

Slocum thought about alerting a store clerk to the shoplifting, then decided against it. From all Pauline had said, any guest was better than one getting tossed in jail. And thoughts of jail sent Slocum's brain off along trails long deserted.

"Benson," he said. "Peter Benson. PB. A sneak thief if ever there was one." Slocum remembered bits and pieces, but enough to make him wonder if Benson—or Benton, as he called himself now—might not be the one who had received Burnside's telegram. He knew nothing of the young telegrapher's background, but it had always struck him as strange that an honest man would ever come up with the notion of so audaciously stealing gold from a bank.

Burnside might have been involved in other crimes, before he came to Slocum with the bank robbery. If so, a man like Peter Benton might have been a part of Burnside's training as a crook. Benton was at least ten years older than Burnside had been, but the telegrapher might have looked on the older man as a mentor.

Slocum shook his head. Burnside was smarter than that. He could have seen through any brag or boast Benton might have made. Still, the coincidence was too great to be ignored. Slocum had run afoul of Benton in a poker game a year or so back. He couldn't remember if it had been Kansas or Indian Territory in a dive along the Mississippi River, but Benton had been cheating and doing a piss poor job of it.

Slocum had caught him and forced him to lose back all the money he had swindled from the other players. Benton hadn't been happy but had gone along with the scheme outlined by Slocum since he hadn't cottoned much to the alternative. Slocum would have plugged him through his thieving black heart if he hadn't lost the money he had stolen.

"Do you remember me, Benton?" Slocum wondered aloud. He shook himself out of the memory of that long ago card game when he saw Pauline waving to him. He hurried on to meet her, leaving Benton to pilfer another store or two before they left.

"John, get the team ready. I found our guests having a late breakfast at the Soda Springs Hotel. They are all fit and ready for the trip." In spite of Pauline's confident words, Slocum heard more than a little worry. He quickly saw why.

Two of the men were more than a little drunk. The other didn't join in their boisterous, bawdy joking but rather closed in on himself like a black storm cloud. The two women in the group reminded Slocum of Adeline Grimsby,—bored, rich, and out for a bit of excitement in their dull socialite lives.

He saw the way they stared at him in their appraising reptilian way, as if wondering what he would cost. Slocum didn't bother telling them they couldn't afford him, at any price.

"I'll fetch the team, and we'll be rolling in ten minutes," he promised. To his surprise, Pauline accompanied him to the stable.

"John, if you want to back out, I won't blame you. I didn't realize they would be drinking so heavily. Lowlanders don't understand the effect altitude has on their ability to consume liquor. But they had friends. Lake House can always use extra guests."

"They're cheap drunks, no matter where they are," he said, leading the four horses from the stable. "I still want to go to Ruxton Park, if your Mr. Benton is going."

"Why, I think so. Yes, there he is. He's the one you want to speak with? Why go up to the Peak?" Pauline looked confused.

Slocum didn't bother telling her that the telegram had preceded them up the mountain. He had no reason even to talk to Benton if he recovered the telegram first. If he could avoid it, why let Benton have an inkling of the fortune that might be awaiting him? Anyway, Benton couldn't demand much, even if Slocum had to buy the telegram from him, because he lacked the information in the other three wires.

As Slocum hitched up the horses, he wondered about Slick Bob Durham's fate. Phil Warren had already high-tailed it out of Colorado, but Durham was a good man, and Slocum hoped he had escaped from the posse so hot to hang him.

"Everybody ready?" he called, mounting the driver's seat. He took the reins in hand, made sure the traces weren't tangled, then got the wagon moving. He liked having Pauline beside him in the box, her leg pressing warmly into his.

"You'll have to show me the road," he told her. "All I'm doing is heading up the canyon."

"There, that's Bear Creek Road. Edward Copley blazed it himself back in '73. The Panic had driven many people bankrupt, and the railroads were threatening to pull out for lack of funds. He bought a tract of land around Lake Moraine for two hundred dollars and started the Lake House Hotel by '74."

The deeply rutted road was easily followed, and Slocum had no trouble getting the horses started up it. But the incline gradually worsened, forcing him to keep working constantly at the team. When the road narrowed and began to parallel a steep cliff, the horses balked.

"We've been going for almost an hour," Slocum said. "The load's wearing the team down. Is there any place for them to rest?" He cast a glance over his shoulder. "I reckon your tourist friends might want to stretch their legs, too."

One of the drunk men had been intermittently sick all the way up the mountain. The other insisted on singing loud and off-key bawdy songs designed to make the ladies blush. Benton said little, and the other man, the one all folded into himself, hardly looked up during the trip.

"Bear Creek widens ahead. Andrew always let the team water and graze for an hour. We're behind schedule, but we still should reach the hotel before sundown. It's not a good idea to be out too long after dark. People have settled in these hills for twenty years, but there's still plenty of wild animals."

With only a six-shooter, Slocum wasn't too anxious to tangle with a cougar or bobcat. He nodded, concentrating on keeping the team moving. Within ten minutes, he saw the deeply rutted area where Andrew had pulled off before.

"Everybody out," called Pauline, jumping to the ground. "We have a picnic lunch." She opened three large baskets Slocum hadn't noticed in the wagon and spread out table-cloths for the guests on the grassy area. He worked at keeping the horses from drinking so much they'd bloat, letting Pauline do the same with her drunken hotel guests. When the horses had finished at the creek, he tied them to pines where they could graze.

He sat and watched as Pauline kept the guests occupied. He had completely misread her. He'd thought she was a fancy lady for a railroad tycoon. Instead, she worked for a living, and damned hard from all Slocum could see.

The meal wasn't for him, so he got up and walked around a bit to stretch his legs. He wandered uphill a hundred yards to check the ever steepening road. Wiping his forehead with his bandanna, he went to the verge of the road and stared down a good hundred yards. If the road hadn't been blasted out of solid rock, he would have worried about the heavily laden wagon being too much for the underpinnings.

The wind whipped through the canyon below, and Slocum lifted his gaze to the towering summit of Pikes Peak. It still carried a cap of snow, but he saw the dark brown thread where the road meandered up its north side. He didn't understand why the rich tourists from Denver wanted to go to the top, but then he didn't understand much about those with more money than he had.

Slocum intended to find out how having too much money turned you crazy.

He grabbed at the brim of his Stetson as a gust of wind blew up from the canyon bottom. Slocum never heard his assailant come up behind, before the rock came smashing down on his head. Slocum tumbled forward, falling over the edge.

10

A sharp pain in Slocum's shoulder brought him to a groggy, vague awareness of his surroundings. He tried to brush away the pain and found new agony lancing into his hand. Slocum shook himself to get the cobwebs from his brain and felt a grating under his body where his gunbelt had caught on a sharp needle of protruding rock. He pulled himself free, then yelped in panic as he started slipping. He came fully awake when he realized he was dangling over the lip of a cliff. A steep cliff. Twisting slightly, he stared down the three-hundred-foot drop to the rocky canyon floor below.

Only then did he figure out the source of the pain in his hand. Clutching at the rock, he fought to keep a vicious crow from pecking at him again. A loud caw told of the bird's displeasure at losing a meal of raw flesh or eye-balls.

"Get away," Slocum croaked, his voice hardly loud enough to be heard over the bird's angry cries. He thrashed about and got another peck on his hand. This forced Slocum to sit up, still clinging to the rock outcropping for support.

He swallowed hard when he realized how close he had come to tumbling over the cliff. Then he sorted out the pains and injuries, remembering the last seconds before he had fallen.

"Someone hit me," he grated. Slocum touched the back of his head and winced. A lump the size of a hen's egg told him how he had come to be hanging on the edge of the mountain. Twisting his head around in spite of the pain, he frowned at the sun's position. It was too early in the day. He had driven for the better part of a morning, and yet it was hardly nine A.M.

Slocum couldn't figure out what was wrong. His first concern was getting up the slope to where he could stretch out without fear of falling to his death. He struggled up the rocky incline, pulled himself over the top, and rolled onto his back, panting hard at the exertion. He was tireder, thirstier, and more confused than ever. When his strength returned, Slocum sat up and looked around for any sign of the wagon, Pauline Yoakum, and her tourists.

He got to his feet and stumbled toward the creek where he had watered the horses. He fell facedown and drank his fill, then washed off the grime and blood he had accumulated. Slocum shouted as the crow came back, trying to peck at his face and eyes. A flailing fist knocked the bird away, convincing it easier meals were available elsewhere.

Slocum got to his feet and studied the ruts in the soft grassy area around the creek. He scratched his head. Where'd they go? he asked himself. These tracks are at least a day old. Then the pieces fell into place. He had lain unconscious on the side of the mountain for a full day. Only catching his gunbelt on a rock had kept him from tumbling to his death.

Slocum started walking uphill and noticed newer tracks, ruts hardly an hour old. He dropped to one knee and measured the width. These hadn't been made by any heavily laden wagon. Slocum guessed they might have been made by a buggy or even a light buckboard pulled by a pair of horses.

"If you saw me on the mountainside and passed me by, you'll pay as dearly as the owlhoot who slugged me," Slocum vowed. He pulled his hat down low on his face to keep the sun out of his eyes, then started hiking in earnest. It was mid-afternoon by the time he reached a grassy meadow stretching up a valley dotted with shimmering, bright lakes.

Slocum carefully studied the road again and saw no sign of other travelers going toward the two-story hotel near the largest of the lakes. He didn't need the freshly painted sign proclaiming this to be the Lake House Hotel to know he had reached his goal. He saw Pauline working at one side of the large structure.

It took him another fifteen minutes of hiking to reach the woman. She didn't see him, being intent on getting the laundry hung. Again it struck him as strange the difference between the woman hanging out laundry and the seductress in the rich surroundings of General Palmer's personal rail car.

"Did you get here in one piece?" Slocum asked. Pauline jumped at the sound of his voice. She turned, her breasts rising and falling with rapid breathing.

"John, it's you. What are you doing here? After you ran off like you did yesterday, I didn't expect to see you again."

"Ran off? Why'd you figure I upped and did a thing like that?" He saw no hint that she was lying or making up a tall tale on the spur of the moment.

"But he said you told him you were—" Her dark eyes widened, then the set he had seen before came to her chin. "Why, that no good, lying son of a bitch!"

"Who?" Slocum couldn't keep from reaching for his six-shooter. He wanted somebody, and Pauline was going to tell him who was responsible for his woes.

"Mr. Benton. He said you told him you were going on ahead on foot, hiking a trail leading to the summit. I thought it was strange, but you *were* gone. Why'd he lie?" Pauline's eyes narrowed now as she stared at Slocum. "What happened, John? You look a fright."

"Someone hit me on the head and threw me over the side of the mountain."

"No!" Pauline's exclamation came out as honest. She was either the best danged actress Slocum had ever seen or she was truly outraged at the treatment he had been given. "I'll talk to Mr. Dana right now. We can put Benton in the shed until the marshal gets up here to arrest him. We can't let him—"

"Don't bother," Slocum cut her off.

Pauline came to him, her fingers tentatively touching his arm. When he didn't pull away, she became bolder. Pauline touched his cheek where the crow had pecked him, then found the lump at the back of his head where he had been hit.

"You're a mess, John," she said. "But I'm glad to see you." She moved even closer, her lips brushing across his. Slocum felt worlds better, though she pulled back and looked sheepish at such a bold kiss.

"Where's Benton?" he asked. Slocum wouldn't have minded staying with Pauline a while longer, but he had more important business with the petty thief. "I'll settle accounts on my own."

"You won't hurt him, will you, John?" Pauline chewed her lower lip, then explained, "We can't afford the bad publicity. If it gets out something like this has happened at Lake House, no one will come. And if you *kill* him . . ."

"I don't remember his real name, but it's not Benton. Might be Benson. Back in Manitou Springs I watched him steal a couple dollars' worth of inventory from the general store. Nothing expensive, but it tells me a whale of a lot about his character."

"How do you know him?" Pauline looked around, as if the Danas would come out and accuse her of loitering. She tugged at Slocum's sleeve, pulling him toward the clotheslines. "I've got to get back to work. There's so much to do, and with only me and—" She swallowed hard. "I've got so much to do."

"I'll let you get to it," Slocum said, wondering what Pauline had almost said. She worked here as a jack of all trades. She'd been about to name someone else and had stopped short of it, as if the mention might bring down the wrath of God on her head. "Just tell me where to find Benton."

"He's with the others out by the lake. That's Mystic Lake," she said unnecessarily, pointing toward the nearby shore. "They took a picnic lunch to the meadow and ought to be about ready to return. You can wait over there."

Slocum didn't intend to sit around waiting for Benton to come back. "I'll be back soon," he told her. "Where can we meet? In the hotel?" He had added the last question to see Pauline's reaction. She turned pale and fought to get the words out.

"That's not a good idea, John. The owners don't like people hanging around who aren't guests or employees. There are hermits all around Ruxton Park, terrible people, some old mountain men who are a little off in the head, they—"

"Where?" he cut her off. "I won't let the Danas see me. I promise."

"Thank you, John." She kissed him as if she meant it, then pushed back and looked guilty again. "Out in the barn. If you don't mind. After dinner. I'll bring you some food, whatever I can. It won't be much but—"

"After dinner," Slocum said. He hitched up his gunbelt and strode off toward the meadow Pauline had indicated. Finding out Benton had been responsible for bushwhacking him came as no real surprise, but he hadn't thought the petty thief had recognized him. Slocum tried to remember when he had crossed trails with Benton before and couldn't put a date on it. Kansas, probably. Some town full of piss and vinegar and more money flowing than any sneak thief could steal using both hands.

But why had Benton tried to kill him? The worst Slocum could have done was make the water a trifle too hot for Benton to swim in. Unless there was more at stake than robbing other guests' rooms and picking pockets.

Peter Benton, Slocum thought as he walked. PB has the telegram, and Burnside must have put more in it than the last clue to the gold. He must have told Benton about me. Slocum tried to reason through Burnside's logic putting so much into a fourth telegram and couldn't. The telegrapher had been dying. This might have been the first telegram he'd sent. The contents of the other three might have been all his dwindling strength could muster.

That didn't seem too sensible, but Slocum didn't have enough information to concoct a better story. He slowed when he heard voices on the soft breeze blowing across the meadow.

He saw the narrow footpath meandering across the grassy area and knew that the picnickers were close. He left the path and went to a stand of trees—a few junipers and even an aspen or two. Slocum loosened the keeper on the hammer of his Colt and started through the trees, moving from shadow to shadow, getting closer to the hotel's lazing guests.

"I cannot wait to begin the trip to the summit," came a female voice. Slocum sneaked a peek around the tree and recognized one of the women who had ridden up in the wagon. The mustached, long-haired man beside her on a blanket wasn't one of the passengers. But another woman spoke, and Slocum knew this was the second woman tourist.

"It's hard to believe the trip to the top of Pikes Peak is only another four miles."

"Four and three-quarter miles," the man corrected, enjoying his display of superior knowledge. "It will be quite a treat getting away from Denver and yet being able to see it. To look down on it and all the little people there, as it were."

This mild joke caused a ripple of amusement. Slocum drifted away, and found another group not ten feet away. They ate quietly, almost intently, their eyes fixed on the ground. The man in black sat with a woman similarly dressed. Slocum wondered if they were allowed ever to chuckle or enjoy the lush Colorado mountain scenery.

Another man hunkered down at the edge of the blanket, picking at his food and looking as if he had chosen the wrong group to dine with.

Slocum heard Benton before he saw him. The man shouted every time he got a stone to skip more than twice across the blue waters of Mystic Lake. Fading back into the grove of trees, Slocum circled and came out on the far side as Benton walked along the shoreline, oblivious to everything but tossing rocks onto the lake. A quick check convinced Slocum he and Benton were hidden by the grove. He slipped his six-shooter from its holster and walked up behind Benton.

"Enjoying yourself?" Slocum asked quietly.

"Decidedly so. I've wanted to—" Benton swung about, realizing nobody had been near when he started around the lake. Seeing Slocum turned his weathered face pale with shock. "You, you can't be here. I—"

"You thought I was dead, didn't you? Now it's your turn." Slocum raised his Colt and cocked it. Benton stared down the muzzle. From his expression it seemed it looked larger than a steam engine.

"Wait. Don't kill me. This is all a mistake, Slocum. I can explain everything." Benton backed off, his hands open and in front of him, as if he could push away any bullet Slocum might send his way. If Slocum fired, there'd be no holding back the slug.

"You obviously know me. That's why you threw me over the side of the mountain," Slocum said.

"It's been a long time since Kansas City," Benton said, "but I couldn't take a chance. I didn't know if you remembered me, but I didn't dare chance it. Really."

"Why not? Because I know you're a sneak thief? I saw you pilfering the needle and thread at the general store. And a knife." Slocum reached out and opened Benton's jacket. The stolen knife had been slid into the lining where the thief could grab it quickly. Slocum plucked it out and tossed it into the lake with a tiny splash.

"You're next. You're going to be fish food, and nobody'll ever find you. Nobody'll even care you're missing, you miserable son of a bitch." Slocum pointed the six-shooter straight at Benton's face, waiting for more information to come flooding out from the trembling lips. If the petty thief got frightened enough, Slocum knew he would spill his guts about everything.

He remembered more of their first meeting after Benton mentioned Kansas City. Slocum had been fresh off a cattle drive, and Benton had made his living robbing drunk drovers. Benton had been a bit too aggressive and had slugged a friend of Slocum's so hard he was never right in the head again. Slocum had run Benton out of town on a rail, and the town marshal hadn't been too upset at all about it.

"This is all I've got, Slocum. Take it. Please, don't kill me. It's not worth wastin' a bullet on me." Benton held out his wallet, hands shaking uncontrollably. Slocum glanced at the leather wallet and saw a few greenbacks stuffed inside. Too few to be worth taking.

"Being a pilferer must not pay too well," Slocum said caustically, lowering his six-gun a mite. He kept it pointed at Benton's midsection. The thin-bladed knife might have been just one of the sneak thief's weapons.

"These folks are *rich*, Slocum. That's why I ponied up the money to come here. They all have more money than they need. One night, two, going through their rooms and I can live for a month!"

"You'd kill me so you could steal a few dollars?" Slocum snorted his contempt for that. He knew why Benton had hit him and tossed him over the cliff.

"Times are hard, Slocum. Really, they are." Benton's face swam in sweat now, and he licked his dried lips constantly.

"How did you meet Burnside?" Slocum asked, tired of Benton's prattling.

"What? Who are you talking about? I don't know any Burnside."

"The telegrapher," Slocum said, his patience wearing thin. "I want the telegram."

"What telegram? I don't know this fellow." Benton's eyes darted left and right, hunting for a way to escape. The lake was on his left and open meadow on his right. His only real chance for hiding lay in the woods, and those were behind Slocum. He would have to get past the deadly six-shooter before finding safety, and that wasn't likely. Not with an able gunman like Slocum.

"What are your initials?" Slocum demanded.

"PB," Benton said. "Peter Benson. I'm only using the name Benton to—"

"I know why you're using a summer name. So the law won't figure out who you are," Slocum said in contempt. Benton could have come up with a better alias than simply changing one letter of his name. "I want the telegram."

"I don't have it!"

"What did Burnside say in it? Tell me and you might live to pick another pocket."

"Slocum, look, it's this way. I—"

The shot caught Benton high in the chest, just below his throat. His legs turned to rubber, and he slipped to the muddy shore of Mystic Lake, as dead as the fish washed up beside him.

Slocum blinked in surprise and stared at the muzzle of his pistol. The Colt Navy had a hair trigger, but he hadn't realized he had fired. Then Slocum knew the truth. The shot had come from behind him, in the woods. He dropped into a crouch and swung about.

He had been so close to getting Benton to tell him what had been in the telegram, so close to recovering the stolen gold, and it had been snatched away at the last possible instant.

When Slocum caught the murderer, he wasn't going to be any too friendly.

11

Slocum was exposed by the lake. He stayed in a gun-fighter's crouch for a moment, waiting to see if another slug would come his way. He wasn't sure if Benton had been the intended victim or if the bullet had strayed a few inches from a target on the back of his head. Either way, Slocum had to be careful.

When no new rounds were fired, he ran toward the woods, straining to pick up the sound of feet running through the soft thatch of needles and leaves on the ground. He entered the cool shadows and immediately swung about, putting a tree trunk to his back and listening hard. He heard distant sounds, possibly someone walking fast, but he couldn't be sure.

Knowing he had only a few seconds or he would lose his quarry completely, Slocum plunged into the midst of the trees, not worrying about the noise he was making. If anything, he hoped the sounds of pursuit might spook the killer into committing a mistake. Slocum was out of breath from running at the high altitude when he came to the far edge of the woods. Stretching for hundreds of yards before him was empty meadow, lush and green and deceptively peaceful.

Where'd I lose him? Slocum wondered. He stepped from the wooded area and looked around. He saw a shallow ravine that he had missed before, running across the mead-ow. If anyone from the grove had entered it, he could make his way back toward the hotel unseen.

Slocum started in that direction and immediately found evidence someone had come by recently. Deep footprints in the muddier sections of the ravine showed that a man had run along. Slocum tried to estimate height and weight and couldn't. The stride was only a little longer than his normal one, yet the imprint was half again as deep.

Short and fat or just slow-walking and confident? Slocum wondered. He kept bent low as he made his way along the ravine. The deep furrow ran near the Lake House, but the footprints didn't go to the hotel. Slocum turned more cautious when he saw that Benton's murderer had gone directly to the barn.

Horses neighed inside, as if someone were preparing for a speedy getaway. Slocum boldly went to the barn door, listened for a moment to be sure he didn't walk straightaway into a trap, then spun around and leveled his gun. The dim interior caused him a moment's blindness, but his eyes adjusted rapidly. And when they did, he saw who was squarely in his gun sights.

"Grimsby!" he exclaimed. "Slocum here."

Hector Grimsby lifted his hands and stepped away from the horse he had been trying to saddle. The man had made a botch of it, the cinches too loose and the horse already aware of who the master would be if anyone mounted. Grimsby would have been thrown off before he'd gotten out of sight of the hotel.

"That was a hell of a good shot you made," Slocum complimented. He moved so that he was inside the barn, a sturdy wall to his back to keep anyone from coming up behind him. "Or was it?"

"What do you mean, Slocum?" The hardware magnate's rotund face rippled with emotions Slocum couldn't put a name to, even if he'd wanted to try.

"Were you aiming at Benton or at me?" To his surprise,

Slocum wasn't unduly upset at this turn of events, though it made getting the telegram more complicated. He wasn't sure if Benton had been telling the truth for a change, about knowing nothing of Burnside's wire, or if the sneak thief had been playing for time.

"Benton, I wanted to kill Benton!" blurted Hector Grimsby. "There's no reason for me to shoot you, Slocum. And I wouldn't do it in the back. Honest."

Slocum wasn't sure Grimsby had ever done an honest act in his life, and that included saying he would never shoot a man in the back. Whether Grimsby knew about Slocum and Adeline Grimsby's assignation counted a lot toward determining the man's candor. Slocum didn't doubt Grimsby was capable of murder if he thought he was being cuckolded or cheated in a business deal. Back at the Barker House he had certainly been willing to engage in a duel with a man he had just met.

"How do I know that?" asked Slocum. In spite of losing his link to the telegram in Peter Benton, he found Grimsby's pleading curious. Slocum ought to have been mad. Instead, he was more interested in prying into Grimsby's behavior and motives for killing Benton.

"It's true. I wanted him dead. I came up here intending to shoot him. You have no idea what kind of a man he was."

"I know what he was," Slocum said cautiously. "Why don't you tell me what he was."

"He was a damned blackmailer, that's what he was! He was milking me for every cent I have. I couldn't let him ruin my reputation." Grimsby's indignation made Slocum wonder if the man might not be telling the truth. This was such a twisted motive it might be true.

"What did he hold over you?" Slocum lowered the six-shooter and waited for an answer.

Grimsby hemmed and hawed a few seconds before blurting, "I won't tell you. If I did, you'd just take Benton's place and blackmail me, too."

"Not interested," Slocum said, wondering what Benton

might have found out about the hardware store owner. For Grimsby to work up the gumption to kill him, it must have been enough to send Grimsby away to Canon City Penitentiary for a long, long time. Slocum couldn't think of any sexual peccadilloes Grimsby wouldn't be willing to fess up to or even brag about, even in front of his wife.

"What are you going to do? Turn me in to the authorities?" Grimsby sweat like a hog, and Slocum knew he had him squarely in his hip pocket. But what did he gain by this power? All Slocum wanted was the telegram, and he couldn't see how Grimsby could help him recover it.

"There's no call to do that," Slocum said, wondering if he ought to try a little blackmail of his own. Murder would provide a powerful lever for any man in Grimsby's position. But Slocum didn't cotton much to men who crept around in the night, whispering dirty secrets. He did his fighting in the open where everyone could see it. There had been things in his life he had done that he wasn't too proud of, but he never denied doing them.

"You won't tell? They'll find the body and suspect me." Grimsby wasn't thinking too clearly.

"Why would anyone think you had it in for Benton? More likely, they'd think you were gunning for me." Slocum considered simply taking one of the horses and riding away from Ruxton Park. The land was lush and pretty, but the people were treacherous and he was leaving a trail of corpses behind him. Andrew and his girlfriend in Manitou Springs. Now Peter Benton dead on the lakeshore. And these were only the ones since he'd started hunting for the telegram.

"I don't hold anything against you. That was a fair fight," Grimsby said, and Slocum knew the hardware salesman was lying.

"Why, there you are," came a woman's voice from behind Slocum. He hastily holstered his Colt and half turned to see Adeline Grimsby in the barn door. Her face split into a wide grin when she recognized Slocum with her husband.

"As I live and breathe, if it isn't Mr. Slocum. I wondered if we would see one another again." She came up and rubbed against him in her suggestive manner. Slocum felt unclean and moved away, again considering leaving and forgetting about the gold.

Twenty-five thousand dollars' worth of gold. Maybe that much in greenbacks. And it would be his if he found it. Warren had forsaken his share, Burnside was dead, and Slocum had no idea what had become of Slick Bob Durham. By Slocum's lights, if they joined up again, Slick Bob was due his share.

He was going to stay, in spite of Adeline Grimsby.

"I came to fetch you, Hector. It's time for afternoon tea. And you are coming, too, aren't you, Mr. Slocum?" Adeline Grimsby tugged hard on his arm, almost dragging him toward the Lake House. He didn't know how to tell her he wasn't a guest, so Slocum let her pull him until he could get free.

Luckily, Pauline Yoakum rescued him.

"Mr. Slocum," she said, her alert, dark eyes darting from Adeline Grimsby to Slocum and back to the woman, "what a coincidence finding you here. I need your help for a few minutes."

"Oh, you can't take him from us, dearie. We were on our way to that marvelous tea Mrs. Dana set out for the *guests*." Adeline Grimsby clung like a leech to Slocum's arm and cut off the circulation. Slocum heard Hector Grimsby snorting like an angry bull behind him. Slocum pulled free, and twisted about, so that when Adeline grabbed to regain her hold, she ended up with her husband's arm.

"I thought that matter had been taken care of," Slocum said to Pauline, playing along with her. "I'll be at the tea in a few minutes, Mrs. Grimsby."

"Oh, be sure you are or I'll come looking for you." Adeline Grimsby made a face she must have thought was cute or seductive or both. Slocum fought to keep his face neutral.

The Grimsbys walked toward the hotel, arm in arm. Pauline said in an irritated voice, "What is all that about? I've seen bulldogs with less powerful bites."

Slocum considered what he ought to tell Pauline. She didn't own the Lake House or even run it. But he felt he could trust her. He just wasn't going to go into the frantic minutes he'd spent with Adeline Grimsby back at the Barker House Hotel.

"One of your guests is going to turn up missing," Slocum said.

"Benton?" Pauline chewed at her lip, then asked, "Did you kill him?"

Slocum laughed and shook his head. "Grimsby did. I'm not sure if he was aiming to plug me in the back and missed or if he really wanted to gun down Benton. Either way, Benton is dead out on the shore of Mystic Lake."

"This is going to ruin business when the sheriff finds out," Pauline moaned. "He'll raise a ruckus and cause so much bad publicity. I don't think he much likes Mr. Copley. We're having enough trouble getting tourists to come this way."

"You told me about that." Slocum saw the imposing summit of Pikes Peak and wondered what possessed the rich guests to go to the top. "Unless you've got something more important to do right now, let's go out to the lake and get rid of Benton's body. Nobody'll notice he is gone. If anyone asks after him, you can always say he took off on a side trip of his own."

"I suppose he won't be missed, if what you said about him is true." The way Pauline stared at him made Slocum wonder if she believed Grimsby was the killer.

"We had met once before, in Kansas City." Slocum went on to tell Pauline about the sneak thief's actions. By the time he'd finished with the story and relating how Benton had slugged him to keep from being exposed, they had reached the shore.

Benton's body was halfway into the lake, giving Slocum

an idea. "Is there a boat around here? We can put a few rocks in his pockets and dump him in the middle of the lake."

"There's a dock a quarter mile farther along. What of the guests? They were picnicking around here somewhere."

"Back there. Why don't you tell them it's teatime and hustle them back to the hotel?"

"A good idea." Pauline stopped and stared into Slocum's green eyes. "John, how can I thank you for all you're doing? You're saving not only my job but the hotel's reputation."

"I can think of a way," Slocum said. Pauline's eyes jerked away, and she shook her head. Tears formed in the corners of her eyes and her shoulders quaked, as if she held back an immense tide of emotion.

"I can't do that, John. Please don't ask. You don't understand."

"Don't get me wrong," Slocum said hurriedly. He didn't know what was going on inside Pauline's head. She obviously found him as attractive as he did her, but the woman was backing off with great reluctance. "Since Benton's room isn't going to be used, let me have it for a night. I'll clear out when I finish my business."

"That's all you want, John?" She turned back to him, her eyes welling with unshed tears.

How he wanted to recover the gold and offer to share it with her!

"For the moment," he said. "Now, get moving and herd those tourists back to the Lake House. I've got work to do."

Pauline surprised him by bending over and giving him a fleeting kiss that started on his cheek and then brushed across his lips like the wings of a butterfly. Then the beautiful woman dashed off toward the grove to find the picnickers.

Slocum tried to sort out her reactions as he hiked along the shoreline. He couldn't do it. He finally found the dock and the small rowboat tied to it. Slocum took longer rowing back to where Benton's body lay than he had walking. It required more skill than he had working the oars. Slocum finally splashed out and wrestled the body into the bottom of the small boat.

He fetched enough rocks from along the lake to weigh down Benton's body, then rowed to the center of the lake, where he judged it to be deepest. Then he loaded Benton's pockets and finished a distasteful chore, using a scaling knife he found in the bottom of the boat. Slocum slit open Benton's belly to keep the decay gases from floating the body to the surface in a day or two.

Then he heaved Benton to his eternal rest at the bottom of Mystic Lake.

Slocum washed off his hands, tossed the scaling knife into the lake, and started rowing back to the dock. By the time he reached the Lake House, he was dog tired and ready to find Benton's room and sleep a few hours.

Slocum was denied that when Adeline Grimsby came running up to him. "Mr. Slocum, you're just in time to join us."

"Sorry, I'm a mess. Let me go to my room and change clothes." Slocum hoped Pauline would hear his plea and come rescue him. He needed the key to Benton's room, and he wasn't going to ask the manager for it. That would cause questions to be asked he didn't want to answer.

"Nonsense. You can join us. No one will care." Adeline Grimsby pulled him along like a small child. Slocum saw the way Hector Grimsby glared at him, but the others were equally antagonistic. They had to recognize him as their driver and must have wondered why Adeline insisted on inviting him to their formal tea.

The tables had been set with linen tablecloths and fine bone china. A plate of tiny sandwiches without crusts sat in front of each guest, and cups of tea had been poured but not many consumed yet. Adeline Grimsby shoved Slocum down in a chair beside her and moved to serve him.

"Mr. Slocum and I are old friends," she said, more for

her husband's benefit than for the others at the table.

"And Hector and I go back a ways, too," Slocum said. Grimsby grunted and nodded, about all Slocum could have hoped for. The two women who had been on the picnic whispered to each other behind their gloved hands, and the men with them seemed more interested in a document they pored over than their women or the tea.

Slocum felt the tense undercurrents flowing around him, and they weren't caused by the Grimsbys. He wondered what he had blundered into, and how long it would take to get free.

12

Slocum finally got away from Adeline Grimsby and the tea party when Pauline came out and bent over to tell him in a voice just loud enough to be heard by the others, "Mr. Slocum, we need to speak about your room."

"Is there a problem?" Slocum asked, realizing Pauline was giving him a way out of Adeline Grimsby's iron grip. "It's not that broken spring in the bed, is it?"

"I'm afraid so. We need to take care of it and make an adjustment to your bill." Pauline tried to look apologetic. To Slocum's way of thinking, she looked more sly than repentant, but he must have been the only one to think so. Adeline Grimsby reached over and touched his arm when she spoke.

"Oh, Mr. Slocum, do see about this tedious problem and return. We have so much to talk about, but I know you wouldn't want anything like a broken spring to disturb your . . . sleep."

"I'll be back when I can," he said, mentally adding that it would be when hell's hinges rusted shut.

"We won't be long," Pauline assured him and led him off to the hotel lobby. Slocum followed quickly, ducking into the dim, cool interior. He paused a moment, looking around.

The lobby wasn't as posh as the Barker House's, but the Lake House Hotel was twelve miles up the mountainside and intentionally rustic. Still, it was more luxurious than Slocum had expected. He waited for the sound of an outraged owner or manager demanding to know what this saddle bum was doing in the hotel, but Pauline had chosen her time well. The desk clerk was gone, and through a partially opened door Slocum saw a man and woman poring over a ledger book.

"Those are the Danas," Pauline told him in a whisper. "Here, take this." She pressed a room key into his hand and quickly started up a staircase on the far side of the lobby. Slocum wasted no time going after her. At the top of the creaking stairs stretched a long corridor, the guest rooms on either side. Slocum held up the room key and saw that Benton had been in Room 13.

It hadn't been a lucky number for the sneak thief. Slocum hoped that Benton's death had changed his luck. He needed to get the telegram and escape Adeline Grimsby.

Pauline stood in the doorway and gestured urgently to him. He didn't hesitate in joining her. She pushed him into the room and closed the door behind him. He looked around and saw that this wasn't Benton's room. It had the look of being more permanent than a guest room, and Slocum wondered if it was Pauline's.

"I don't have much time, John," she told him. "Benton's room is down the hall. I can't remember him too well, but I doubt his clothing would fit you. Take this." She thrust a carpetbag into his hands. "Something in there will fit, I think."

"Thank you," he said. "Especially for getting me away from Adeline Grimsby."

Pauline made a face. "She has tried to seduce every man at Lake House, everyone except her husband." Pauline's expression altered slightly when she asked, "Do you know her?"

"We met in Manitou Springs," he said, "and it was not

a pleasant experience for me."

Pauline started to say something more, perhaps to ask for details. She shook her head, causing a small disarray of her raven's-wing dark hair to float about her face in a filmy halo. The sun caught her high cheekbones and broad forehead just right, turning her into an angel. Slocum wanted to reach out, take her in his arms, and kiss her.

But he didn't. He remembered her unwillingness even to suggest such a possibility happening again. Slocum wished he knew more about her, but until Pauline told him, he wasn't likely to find out—and he wasn't going to pry. He had better things to do.

The lure of gold was strong, and the telegram had been delivered to Lake House. If Benton hadn't received the wire, someone else had—or the telegram was still in the desk clerk's file. If so, Slocum could start spending the money right away.

"Pauline, I need you to—" His request for her to check for the telegram was cut off when she raised an index finger to her lips, silencing him.

He heard heavy footfalls out in the hall. From her frightened expression, he thought she must have expected Benton to have risen from the bottom of Mystic Lake and come to accuse her of killing him.

"You've got to go before someone finds you in here." Pauline opened the door a crack, peered outside fearfully, then pushed Slocum into the hall. "Benton's room is at the end of the corridor. I'll talk to you later."

Slocum slipped from the room and hurried to Benton's room. The key slid into the lock and opened the well-oiled door. This room was more what he expected in a guest room. While clean and well appointed, the furnishings lacked the personal feel apparent in the room he had just left.

Slocum went to the window and studied the grounds. He had a good view of the lake, and the barn was just barely in sight in the opposite direction. Because he was at the end of the corridor, there was no room next to his on the lake side, but there was an exterior door and a flight of well-kept stairs leading down to the grassy grounds. This suited Slocum just fine. He could come and go without having to pass a clerk in the lobby, who might ask why this Mr. Benton looked nothing like the one who had registered earlier.

Onto the bed he dumped the contents of the carpetbag Pauline had given him and rummaged through what he found. Some of the clothing was finely tailored, while some shirts were threadbare. From the varied pieces and quality, Slocum figured Pauline had given him duds left behind by any number of forgetful or negligent guests. He held up one white shirt with a ruffled front and decided that it might be better worn by a high stakes professional riverboat gambler than a guest at the Lake House. Slocum discarded the frilly shirt for a plainer one, and skinned out of his clothing and into it. A pair of pants, a tad too tight across the bottom but fine in length, finished his basic attire.

A full-length mirror on the back of the door let him study himself carefully.

"Not so bad. I'm not the clothes horse most of the men at this hostelry are, but this is passable." Slocum used water from the pitcher on the dresser to rinse out his own clothing and then hung it up to dry. He finished his washing by making sure all traces of Benton's blood were off his hands. Only then did he fall on the soft bed and stare up at the ornately worked plaster on the ceiling.

He was tired, more tired than he could remember being in a coon's age, but sleep wouldn't come. The soft bed, the gentle breeze blowing through the window, the lulling sounds of wind moving through distant tall pines—none of it soothed him into a much needed sleep. His mind kept turning over the unanswered questions plaguing him.

Who had killed Andrew and his girlfriend back in Manitou Springs? Slocum hadn't even seen Benton then, nor had he locked horns with Hector Grimsby. If it had been the deputy from Denver—Tom—why give up after a few shots? The deputy would have kept after him until one or the other of them was dead. He wouldn't have fired three or four times and simply walked away.

And there was the matter of PB. Benton had claimed not to know anything of the telegram. His expression had turned cagey at the mention of Matt Burnside's name, but Slocum thought that was only because Benton saw a way out of his predicament. Confidence men used slips of the tongue to make hundreds of dollars. Benton might have seen this mention as nothing more than a wedge to get free of Slocum.

If Benton wasn't the PB Burnside had sent the telegram to, who was? Slocum didn't feel any closer to answering that question, not that it mattered much to him. He had three clues and needed only one more to retrieve the gold. Even if PB knew what his telegram meant, without the other three clues he had nothing.

Slocum wasn't against splitting the take from the bank robbery with this mysterious PB if that was what it took to get back the stolen gold, but the entire stash was better than taking on a new partner.

Slocum heaved himself out of the bed and settled his gunbelt around his waist. He slipped into the hall, went down the back stairs, and moved around to the side of the hotel until he could peer through a lobby window. He saw that the desk clerk was gone and the lobby stood as empty as a drummer's promise. The guests had gathered in the dining room, with the staff serving them.

Taking this as a good sign, Slocum hurried around and into the lobby. The door to the dining room was open, but Slocum walked quickly in front of it and vaulted over the narrow counter to the wooden niches holding keys and letters. He scanned the mailboxes for any sign of a telegram. Not finding one, he started going through the mail, hunting for anyone with the proper initials.

Disgusted when he failed to find anyone with PB as

part of his name, Slocum jumped back over the counter and went up the stairs to the guest rooms. They stretched along the corridor on either side. Slocum started on his left side, jiggling and rattling a doorknob until the simple lock yielded.

Slocum almost backed out when he recognized Adeline Grimsby's clothing in the wardrobe. He forced himself to search through the bags and steamer trunk for any correspondence. Slocum found a bundle of letters packed in lavender. Leafing through them quickly, he saw nothing to waste his time on. Let Adeline Grimsby keep love letters from her admirers. Slocum didn't have to check to see that no two were from the same man, and none were from her husband.

He left and went across the hall, repeating the rattling and pressure until the door yielded. This room had a sparser array of belongings in it, probably belonging to the quiet man who dressed all in black and kept to himself. Slocum considered him a prime candidate for being PB. But he soon found that the man's name was Samuel Schliecker, a consumptive who had come from New York City for his health.

Slocum let out a sigh. This was taking longer than he had thought. He might have to risk breaking into the rooms after the tourists had retired for the night. That was dangerous, but Slocum felt an increasing pressure of time weighing him down. He went to the next room, saw that it was Pauline's, and started to burgle the room across the hall.

He froze when footsteps echoed up the creaking stairs. Slocum twisted hard at the doorknob and found that it was securely fastened. He spun back to Pauline's room and tried this knob. To his relief the door wasn't locked. He ducked into the room and shut the door as two people came down the hall.

Outside, it had turned inky dark, without a moon to light the mountain meadows of Ruxton Park. Slocum tried to open the window but couldn't get it to budge.

"I don't want to discuss it," came Pauline's troubled voice outside the door.

"Inside. We'll get it out in the open right now," came the grating reply. The door creaked as someone kicked at it.

Slocum couldn't get out the window in time. He grabbed at the wardrobe door and ducked inside an instant before Pauline and a man burst into the room. The man shoved Pauline onto the narrow bed. She landed facedown. Before she could turn over, the burly man dropped beside her and grabbed her wrists, pinning her.

"You stupid bitch," he shouted. "You're holding out on me. You can't tell me that's all you have."

"It is, it is," sobbed Pauline. She fought to get free, but the man was too strong for her. He half stood, then dropped with his knee in the middle of her back. She cried out in pain.

"I ought to beat you within an inch of your life," he snarled.

Slocum opened the wardrobe door slightly. He hesitated when he saw Pauline. Opening the door a little more gave him a clearer view of the man sitting atop Pauline, even if all he could see was the back of the man's head. The man's fist was cocked back. Slocum's hand went to his six-shooter, but he didn't draw.

And he immediately regretted it. The man hit Pauline on the side of the head, stunning her.

"Hold out on me again and you'll regret it." The man struck Pauline once more. Slocum shoved the door to open it, only to get a dress tangled in the catch, preventing him from jumping into the room. The cloth tore and Slocum stumbled forward, his Colt Navy out. But the man had already vanished into the hallway, never seeing Slocum.

"Pauline, are you all right?" He knelt beside her. The woman had been hit just above the right eye. A large purple-and-green bruise had already formed. She moaned and tried to turn away from Slocum.

"Don't hit me again. Please don't."

"Pauline, it's me. Slocum." He rolled her onto her back and saw the other spot where the man had hit her. A deep cut there bled profusely. The man must have worn a heavy ring to inflict such a wound.

"John?" Pauline tried to focus her eyes but found it almost impossible. She touched her forehead and winced. The eye was starting to swell shut. "How'd you get here?"

"Never mind that," he said. "Who hit you? I got a glimpse of him. About my height, heavier, thinning dark hair. Who is he?"

"No, John, don't tangle with him. He's poison. Pure poison!"

Slocum went to the window and stared out across the meadowlands. He didn't see anyone moving, but he heard the door at the end of the corridor, down by his room, slam shut. Slocum strained to see if anyone came down the stairs, but he was on the wrong side of the hotel.

He dashed for the door, even as Pauline called after him, "Don't go after him, John. You don't understand. Please!"

Slocum ignored her. Any man who beat up a woman deserved nothing better than being staked out in the desert for the ants and buzzards. Wasting a piece of lead was almost too good. Slocum raced down the corridor, slammed into the door, and hit the stairs at a dead run.

The man had vanished.

Slocum landed hard at the bottom of the steps and looked around. He saw nothing moving in the darkness, not even the tops of trees. The wind had died, and an unnatural calm had settled on the Lake House Hotel. He went toward the front of the hotel, thinking the man might have gone to rejoin the tourists in the dining room.

Slocum ducked back as he came even with a window. In the lobby, all the guests were laughing, drinking, and enjoying a merry party. Slocum peered in, trying to recognize the man among the male guests. Two were about the right height, but they seemed well on the way to being falling-down drunk. He doubted either could have made it back into the hotel fast enough.

"The stables," he muttered. If Pauline's assailant hadn't gone back into the Lake House, he must have bolted for the barn to escape. Slocum ran for the distant barn and heard the frightened neighing of horses inside. He had been right about the woman-beating son of a bitch's destination.

Slocum jerked open the door and whirled into the barn, Colt leveled and ready to end a miserable life.

The horses in their stalls reared and lashed out with their hooves, creating such a clatter that Slocum didn't hear the footsteps behind him. The first he knew of the man behind him was a shadow falling over his, cast by a lantern high up in the barn.

Slocum dropped to a gunfighter's crouch and tried to get his six-shooter swung around in time. A heavy blow smashed into the side of his head, staggering him. A second wallop knocked him wobbling, falling backward. He crashed into a stall and slid down the wooden wall, stunned. A final blow, on the top of his head, caused the world to slide into total blackness.

13

Slocum felt feathers tickling his cheek. He tried to push them away and only drowned in a sea of red-hot pain. He moaned and rolled to his side. Slocum instantly regretted it. His ribs felt as if they'd been staved in.

"John, please wake up. John, please."

The voice came from the other side of the moon. Slocum struggled to recognize it. The light caresses returned to his cheek, and these brought Slocum out of his blinding haze of pain. He blinked and saw Pauline bending over him.

"Oh, John, are you hurt?"

"Been better," he got out. His head must have been split wide open to cause this much pain. Every breath he took caused his ribs to burn with a fire that wouldn't die down. He gradually put the pieces back together. He had come into the barn after Pauline's attacker and been coldcocked. Two or three blows to the head, and then his attacker must have spent a fair amount of time kicking him in the ribs to cause such torture.

"I was afraid he would kill you. He ran when he heard me coming. He must have thought it was Mr. Dana."

"You know him," Slocum said accusingly, sitting up. He felt a little better, the pain dying down. Pure, cold rage replaced it. The next time he crossed paths with that sidewinder, there would be a new grave to be dug.

"It . . . yes, John, I know him. That's Charley."

"Who the hell is Charley and why is he whipping on you the way he did? No man does that to a woman and gets by with it."

"You're interfering where you don't belong, John," the lovely woman said. Slocum saw the anguish on her face. He also saw the bruises and the way she winced every time she bent. That knee in the small of her back had hurt her badly.

"I might have agreed before Charley slugged me. Now it's *my* business." He slid his Colt Navy back into the cross-draw holster and put the keeper over the hammer.

Slocum's green eyes fixed on Pauline's dark ones. He said softly, "Who is he?"

"My husband," came the startling reply. At first Slocum thought he hadn't heard her right. Then he saw the torment on her lovely face and knew he had.

"Your husband? You married a low-down, no-account woman-beating snake?" Pauline hadn't seemed the kind to up and do such a dumb thing. He had thought she was with the richest man in Colorado, and that had seemed right for her. When Slocum had discovered she worked at a hotel, that had perplexed him. This revelation took him by storm.

"Please, it's not like that. Charley isn't so bad if he's sober. It's just that he never seems to be sober anymore." Pauline sat down in the straw beside him and continued her sorry tale. "I didn't even tell my family, not that I have much left these days. My parents were killed last year in a fire, and—"

"He beat you because you didn't give him enough money," Slocum said in a voice colder than ice.

"Yes," she answered, her voice small and frightened. Pauline turned to him and buried her face in his shoulder. He felt hot, wet tears soaking into his shirt. Slocum didn't know what to do or say. He had made a rule out of never touching another man's wife. Although he hadn't known Pauline was married when he boarded the train in Denver, he was startled to find that he didn't feel much different about her now.

She was still lovely—and desirable. Charley Yoakum was no fit husband.

"How long have you been married?" he asked.

"Only two months, and it's been a horrible mistake. I want to divorce him, John. I can't take any more of his abuse. He calls me names, he beats me. It's terrible."

"If you left him, do you have anywhere to go?"

"I've got a sister back in St. Louis and a brother, but I couldn't intrude on them. They have lives of their own." She looked up from his shoulder, her dark eyes burning with need. Slocum never dallied with married women. In that course lay real trouble.

He kissed Pauline Yoakum hard. And she returned the kiss.

Slocum's principles went flying away as passion mounted. He had never wanted a woman as he did Pauline Yoakum. His hands worked at the buttons on her plain blouse, and then, once the cloth opened, one hand dipped inside to cup her left breast. The woman moaned softly and shoved forward, driving her hardening nipple into his palm.

He was never quite sure how she got him out of his shirt or gunbelt or trousers, but she did. He bent over to kiss and lick at her breasts as she worked discarding his unwanted clothing. His tongue left a wide, wet trail that made Pauline shiver with every touch. When he came to the snowy summit of her right breast, his tongue teased and tormented the coppery nipple until she leaned back, quaking with need.

"More, John," she begged. "I need more than your mouth. I want all of you!"

Her hand closed around his growing hardness and brought it to complete erection. Slocum worked his hands down her sides, passing quickly when she winced in pain. Her husband had injured her back enough to make motion a trial. Slocum intended to give the woman something to make her forget the hurt.

His fingers worked to lift her skirt. He found frilly undergarments and quickly drew them past her slender thighs and off her trim legs. Pauline lay back fully, her breasts glowing in the dim light cast by the lantern above them.

"Now, John, don't wait. I want you now."

And Slocum wanted her, married or not. His hands parted her legs. She opened willingly for him. He wondered if she had ever done so for Charley Yoakum, then forgot the man entirely as he slid forward into paradise. Completely surrounded by warm, clutching female flesh, he shuddered with stark delight.

When he began withdrawing slowly, an inch at a time, it was Pauline's turn to shiver with lust. Her fingers clawed at his shoulders and back as she silently urged him on. Eyes closed and lost in the sensations rippling through her, Pauline uttered not a word until Slocum drove back into her body.

"Oh, yes, yes!" she gasped out. "I need this, John, my love, yes, yes!"

Slocum began a rhythmical stroking that carried him balls-deep into her, then out until only the thick purple head of his shaft remained in her delicate pink nether lips. Pauline's legs rose on either side of his body locking firmly behind his back, as he slipped forward again. Even if he had been foolish enough to want to leave, he couldn't now.

Carnally trapped, Slocum moved faster and faster. His hands brushed across her sensitive breasts and nipples, stroked over her jaw, and even touched the bruise on her forehead. Then his own desires built to the point where he was being consumed.

Placing his hands firmly on the barn floor on either side of her body, Slocum began stronger movements, more powerful inward strokes. He felt the woman responding beneath him. Pauline's dark eyes opened, but they didn't see him. They were glazed with lust as she thrashed about, lifting her hips off the floor to crush down firmly as he entered her. The fire deep in his loins built to a conflagration that totally devoured him.

The white-hot tide rising within him was not to be denied. He grunted, arched his back, and spilled his seed into her yearning interior. He was dimly aware of Pauline's legs pulling him even deeper into her body. She shrieked out her passion and half sat, her body trembling like a leaf and a hot flush rising on her shoulders and neck.

Then Pauline sank back down, covered with sweat. Slocum relaxed and stared down into her lovely face. Never had he found a woman who appealed more to him. What had Charley said or done to make her marry him? Slocum was at a loss to know.

He rolled to one side, and Pauline snuggled into the curve of his arm.

"It's never been this way, John. Not with anyone," she said in a little girl voice. "I like it."

"How did you happen to meet Yoakum?" he asked against his better judgment. He knew he was going to shoot the man. Getting details about his life with Pauline wouldn't make the chore any easier—or harder.

"Mrs. Dana had sent me into Denver. Charley was unlike any man I'd ever seen. My parents had just died and he said all the right things. It wasn't long after we were . . . married that I found out about him."

"That he liked to beat up women?"

Pauline smiled ruefully. "More than that. He'd robbed a couple banks in his day." Slocum perked up when he heard this. "I knew how the Danas felt about ex-convicts, but it didn't matter to me. Not then."

"You got him a job? What does he do around here? I hadn't seen hide nor hair of him until he came to your room."

Pauline sighed and snuggled even closer. "He does odd jobs. He goes into Manitou Springs for supplies sometimes, when Andrew is with a group going to the top of Pikes Peak."

Slocum cut her off with a sharp question. "Did he pick up telegrams for the guests?"

"Sometimes. Why, John? Is that important?" She turned around and looked deep into his eyes. He felt as if she read his very soul. Pauline reached out to touch his cheek. "You're a hard man, too," she said, "but not like Charley."

"Would you be disappointed if you found I'd robbed a bank?" he asked, fearing the answer.

"No, not really. It's not right, but I suspect my brother has had some shady dealings, too. He's always looking for an angle, and I know he does some things that are illegal. I can read him like a book."

"I want to talk with him sometime," Slocum said. "We might have a mutual interest." Pauline stared at him curiously but said nothing more. She lifted her lips to his and kissed softly. Before Slocum realized what was happening, they were making love again.

He came awake with a start when a rooster crowed. Slocum shook Pauline awake and said, "We've got to get dressed. It's daylight. We don't want the manager to find us like this. You'd lose your job for sure." And, Slocum silently added, he might lose his chance to track down Charley Yoakum. Dressing hurriedly, he settled the gunbelt around his waist and made sure the Colt rested easy.

"I've got to get the food prepared for the tourists. They're heading on up to the Peak today," Pauline told him. He asked about the procedure. "It's simple," she explained. "There's a corral behind the barn with a dozen burros. They'll ride to the top, have a lunch, then ride back. It's only five miles to the top, but the going is steep. Without the burros, these tenderfeet wouldn't be able to stumble along, much less walk."

"Part of their anatomy is going to be sore, unless I miss my guess," Slocum said. He couldn't imagine Adeline Grimsby sitting on a burro all day long to reach the fourteen-thousand-foot summit. Picturing Hector Grimsby astride a burro was even more ludicrous.

"They're supposed to leave in about an hour," Pauline said, staring out the barn door at the sun just poking above the mountains. "What are you going to do, John?"

"Find Charley Yoakum," he said. "Where would he spend the night?"

Pauline's lips thinned, and her jaw got a set to it like granite. "Unless one of the women invited him into her bed, which is where he'd prefer to stay, he usually camps out in the woods a half mile north of here."

"He's a fool. I spent the night the right way." Slocum kissed Pauline and then left, intent on tracks in the soft ground. He passed the corral filled with braying burros and headed north. Once, he stopped and looked around, uncomfortable and not knowing why. He doubled back to make sure no one trailed him. He couldn't be sure.

He circled and slowly turned back toward the north and a stand of trees that would afford Charley Yoakum good cover. Slocum worried that he hadn't asked Pauline for a better description of the man. He had seen him from behind and through a narrow slit as he opened the wardrobe door. By the time he had piled out and into the room, Yoakum had vanished. And Slocum had no idea about the man who had slugged him. He reckoned it had to have been Yoakum.

Or was it someone else? He hadn't crossed paths with Yoakum yet in Manitou Springs. Slocum had never figured out who had tried to drygulch him and shot Andrew and his girlfriend by mistake.

A flash of sunlight off metal caught Slocum's eye. He dove for cover and moved forward slowly, creeping up on an abandoned campsite. The fire pit was cold, and the bedroll had been used but not rolled up. Debris from a sparse breakfast of canned beans and peaches lay to one side. But Slocum saw nothing of Charley Yoakum.

Circling, he made sure he wasn't overlooking the man, that he hadn't gone into the woods to take a piss. Where Yoakum had gone, Slocum didn't know. But this presented him with a sterling opportunity. Slocum slipped into camp and quickly searched the bedroll for the telegram.

Nothing.

Saddlebags, he thought, smiling broadly when he spotted them hanging from a tree limb a few feet away. He opened the thong on the side of the saddlebags and rummaged through the contents, hunting for the flimsy yellow paper a telegram would have been recorded on. Yoakum had nothing in his saddlebags to show he had received the fourth clue from Matt Burnside.

As he turned, Slocum caught the glint of sunlight off metal again. This time he recognized a rifle barrel. He jerked sideways, crying out in pain as he strained his bruised ribs. Slocum had moved barely in time. A splinter of wood flew from the tree limb at the level of his head. If he hadn't moved, his brains would have been blown out.

He landed hard and rolled over, pulling out his six-shooter. Slocum got to cover behind a fallen log and fired twice in the direction of the flash he had seen. There wasn't the *feel* of a good shot, and Slocum knew he had missed. Scrambling to his feet, he got into the deeper woods and went hunting.

He hunted for the back-shooter and lost him. Slocum found a spent shell casing and crushed weeds where the sniper had stood, but the would-be killer had evaporated.

"I owe you another one, Yoakum," Slocum said under his breath. He didn't like the idea of cutting across the open, grassy meadow returning to Lake House, but he had no choice. To his surprise, he saw neither Yoakum nor anyone else until he was almost at the corral.

The loud braying carried for some distance as the burros were saddled and prepared for the trail. Slocum slowed as he came up to the corral, where two men talked. He immediately recognized Hector Grimsby. The other man was tall and heavyset.

Slocum didn't know for certain, but he had the feeling this was Charley Yoakum.

He got closer and heard Grimsby saying, "We can get the loot later. Nobody'll be the wiser."

"The robbery—" Yoakum clamped his mouth shut when he realized Slocum could overhear them. He turned away from Grimsby and cinched a saddle tighter around a burro.

Grimsby frowned and then saw the reason for the sudden shift in Yoakum's attention. Grimsby frowned at Slocum, started to say something, then rushed off to talk with his wife. Adeline Grimsby waved gaily and called to Slocum.

He tipped his hat, but his attention centered on the man he thought was Charley Yoakum. What dealings did he have with Grimsby? And what loot were they talking about? Slocum didn't know, but he wanted to find out.

14

"Everyone get mounted. If you need any help, me or my wife'll be glad to help."

Slocum watched Charley Yoakum as he checked each burro and gave a bit of aid to one of the women, whose eyes were only for Yoakum. Yoakum's hands, one adorned with a large gold ring, lingered longer than they ought to have on the woman's waist, and his hand brushed places that would get him called out if the woman's husband noticed. Slocum wasn't sure which man belonged to the woman, but he was sure about Pauline Yoakum.

The beautiful, dark-haired woman came from the Lake House in time to see what her husband was doing. Her face flushed, and she started to call out in disappointment. Instead, Pauline bit her lower lip and turned away, so she wouldn't have to watch. If Slocum had needed any further proof that this was her husband, he had it.

"There we go, Mrs. Grimsby," Pauline said, trying to get Adeline Grimsby settled English-style onto the narrow saddle. The older woman fought Pauline's attempts to get her hiked up onto the burro's back. The sturdy animal brayed and shifted under the uneven weight as Adeline Grimsby slid off.

"You simply don't know what you are doing, my dear,"

Adeline Grimsby said tartly. She turned in Slocum's direction. "Would you please help me, Mr. Slocum? I know you're on vacation, also, but you seem ever so much more competent than these . . . servants."

Slocum restrained himself. He didn't go around hitting women, as Charley Yoakum did. But Adeline Grimsby had given him a good reason to start. She had no call to insult Pauline the way she had, simply to get Slocum to pay more attention to her.

"Your husband's a seasoned rider," Slocum said insincerely, wondering if Hector Grimsby would last an hour on the burro. He already twisted about, trying to find a comfortable seat. "He'll be more than happy to help you mount."

"But it's your mount that I enjoyed," Adeline Grimsby said, her voice just loud enough for Slocum and Pauline to hear. The woman seemed not to care if Pauline eavesdropped. If anything, she might have found it exciting to tease Slocum in such a fashion with her double meanings in front of a woman as pretty as Pauline.

"Let's move out!" Charley Yoakum shouted and lifted his hand high in the air, then motioned for the line of burros to start up the steep mountainside as if he headed a hundred Conestogas crossing the prairie. The tourists chuckled and even laughed, enjoying the notion that they were pioneers.

"You need any help?" Slocum asked Pauline. The woman's eyes were filled with tears. She shook her head.

Slocum swung around and saw that Charley Yoakum had returned once he got the line of tourists moving. Slocum's hand twitched, but he didn't draw his Colt. This man had slugged him and then shot at him—and he had beaten Pauline. Any of these crimes would have been good enough in court to justify Slocum putting a bullet or two through his foul heart.

"You needin' any help . . . Mr. Slocum, is it?" Yoakum cocked his head to one side and studied Slocum hard. This was the first time the two of them had come face-to-face.

"We got to reach the halfway point before noon or we'll never get all the way to the summit today."

Slocum hesitated. He had no intention of going to the top of Pikes Peak, yet Yoakum obviously considered him one of the tourists and encouraged him to ride with them. Slocum had a burro, as did Pauline. He saw the woman finish stowing supplies on four pack burros and mount one of her own.

Slocum made a quick decision. The man—or men—who had shot at him in the woods were most likely on their way to the summit. If he wanted to find out the contents of Matt Burnside's telegram, he had to stay with the group. There was one other reason to go. Pauline was headed up to the Peak, also.

"Just making sure the cinches were tight," Slocum said, swinging onto the small animal's back. His feet almost dragged the ground on either side, but the burro had no trouble with his weight. A single snort of complaint at having a human on its back again was the only sign that the burro cared about or even noticed Slocum. The sure footed animal started off, without Slocum needing to guide it with the reins.

When Yoakum thought Slocum was out of earshot, he snapped at his wife, "Don't go makin' eyes at him. He's a snoop, and I don't like him one little bit."

"Please, Charley, let's just worry about the tourists. We're starting out too late to ever make it to the top before it gets dark." Pauline fell silent when Yoakum growled.

Slocum twisted around and saw Yoakum's fist cocked back, about to strike her again. The man lowered his hand when he felt Slocum's cold eyes fixed on him. Yoakum jerked his burro around and got it moving at a brisk walk, quickly passing Slocum.

Pauline caught up with Slocum and said in a low voice, "Please, John, don't make him mad. Charley has a terrible temper."

"Doesn't even have to be drunk to hit you, does he?"

"John, I don't want to stay married to him, but right now, he *is* my husband. That means something to me." Pauline bit her lip again and tugged hard on the reins of the pack animals, keeping them moving along so they wouldn't graze on the lush mountain grass on either side of the trail.

That Pauline was married to Yoakum meant something to Slocum, too. Yoakum might be the lowest slime-trailing toad on the face of the earth, but he was still Pauline's husband. And even though he'd done it once already, Slocum vowed again not to fool around with another man's woman. Even if every square inch of his body told him to go ahead.

They rode in silence, Slocum lost in thought and not paying much attention to the vistas opening around him. The higher they got on Pikes Peak, the farther they could see to the east. Colorado City and its small neighbor, Colorado Springs, were tiny dots in the distance. The strange wind-eroded shapes in the Garden of the Gods showed red and wondrous. Slocum thought he could even make out Denver through the distance haze at the end of a gleaming silver ribbon of railroad track.

But their progress was painfully slow thanks to Adeline Grimsby. No matter what her husband did, the woman insisted on getting off her burro every few minutes. And after an hour on the trail, Hector Grimsby began complaining to Yoakum to slow the pace.

Slocum saw that they would never reach the top of the mountain before dark, though it was only five miles distant. He mentioned this to Pauline, who smiled wanly and shook her head. The way her dark hair flowed in the cold wind blowing off the snowcapped summit turned her into an angel.

"We try to reach the summit, since it is so close, but we don't always make it with the greenhorns we herd along."

"The supplies?" Slocum pointed to the pack animals.

"We have enough provisions for two days. Blankets, food, everything to camp under the stars. Most of the tourists enjoy returning to Denver and bragging about how they had to rough it ascending Pikes Peak."

Slocum started to say more, but Yoakum and Hector Grimsby came up to him.

Yoakum glared at Pauline and said, "Get some lunch ready for them." His cold eyes turned to Slocum. He tipped his head off to one side, inviting Slocum to talk in private. Grimsby looked around nervously, giving Slocum the impression he had a distasteful chore to do and wanted it over as fast as possible.

Slocum slipped off his burro, which wandered away to graze at a juicy patch of grass. A marmot popped out of a nearby burrow and chittered loudly at this invasion of its domain, then dove back into its hole when the three men walked past.

"Me and Hector been talkin' about you, Slocum," Yoakum said without preamble once they were a ways from the party of tourists. "Why are you nosin' around?"

"You a lawman?" blurted Grimsby.

Slocum fought to keep from laughing at such an absurd allegation. He shook his head and said, "I've been called a lot of names in my day, but not that one." He saw that Grimsby wasn't convinced, but Yoakum had a better sense of what a lawman might do. Still, Slocum decided to nudge them a bit more.

He stared squarely at Grimsby when he asked, "What loot were you two talking about back at the corral?"

"Why, I . . . we didn't . . . What loot?" With his expression Grimsby lost any chance of plausibly denying he and Yoakum had been discussing loot from some robbery. Slocum didn't have to be much of a poker player to read the lie all over the fat hardware magnate's face.

"We'll ask the questions," Yoakum cut in. His hand rested on a six-shooter stuck into his belt. Slocum judged how fast Yoakum might draw, and how quick he could get his own Colt Navy into action. He wasn't worried, as long as he faced the man. Experience had taught him to watch his back, though.

Yoakum tried to assert himself, but Slocum wasn't going to let him get an edge. Before the man could press any advantage he thought he might have, Slocum asked, "What happened to the telegram from Burnside?"

For a moment Slocum thought Yoakum knew nothing about any telegram. The man's face sweated like snow melting in the spring sunlight, but then a cunning gleam came to his eye.

"You know something about a telegram?"

"I want to know what's in it. Doesn't do you any good. Together, we might make it pay off big." Slocum dangled the promise of money to see if he could entice an admission out of Yoakum. He had searched the man's gear and not found it. Whether Yoakum had the telegram on him or had memorized it and destroyed it, Slocum had to find out.

"What are you talking about?" asked Grimsby, confused. "I thought he was trying to get us to tell about robbing the—"

"Shut up, Grimsby," snapped Yoakum. "You ain't got the brains God gave a goose."

Whatever loot Grimsby and Yoakum had talked about, Slocum knew now it had nothing to do with the take from the bank robbery. As such, he was no longer interested in finding out about it. All that mattered to him was the gold from the First Denver Bank's vault.

"We're going to have to get the tourists chowed down and back on the trail. There's no way we'll get to the Peak today." Yoakum swung around and stalked off, leaving Grimsby gaping. The corpulent store owner started to speak, then clamped his mouth shut and followed his partner in whatever crime they had committed.

Slocum shook his head. There were too many crooks involved. All he wanted was his due from the robbery. Burnside's telegram had ended up in someone's pocket.

Slocum had thought Yoakum had collected the wires at Manitou Springs and taken them to the Lake House. But had Yoakum read the telegram addressed to PB?

Who the hell was PB?

Slocum joined the tourists, trying to stay away from Adeline Grimsby. He found it impossible. The woman grabbed his arm and held on tighter than any blood leech, much to Hector Grimsby's disgust. But the man said nothing and even seemed to take a satisfaction from it that puzzled Slocum. Slocum wondered if Grimsby still thought he was a lawman come to clap him in the nearest jail. Slocum ate lunch, engaging as many of the others in conversation as he could. This kept Adeline Grimsby at bay. What Slocum wanted most was to talk with Pauline, but the woman worked diligently to feed her wards.

They were on the trail again by mid-afternoon and looking for a place to camp before nightfall. Slocum didn't have a chance to talk to Pauline, though he often let his burro fall back. She worked to avoid him, and he didn't much blame her. It would only cause her pain, and a world of trouble from her husband.

Still, Slocum found it impossible to resist the pretty woman's allure.

"We camp here for the night and finish our trip to the top just after dawn," Yoakum told the tourists. As Pauline had hinted, this delay pleased the paying customers more than it frightened them. The altitude was such that strenuous walking was difficult for them, but the burros took all the work out of getting to the summit of Pikes Peak.

Slocum saw that Charley Yoakum let his wife unload all the blankets. Slocum was tempted to help, but a glint of sunlight against metal from farther down the mountain caught his attention. Looking around, he saw Grimsby and Yoakum heading off to the west, circling the mountain until they vanished into a deep ravine.

"Need any help?" Slocum asked Pauline, staring past the woman at the trail they had just covered.

"I could use some once everyone gets a blanket or two. Most of them have some idea how to make a bed," Pauline said lightly. "I've got sheets of canvas. Some of them might like to find a limb and drape the canvas over to give them privacy."

"I'll be back to do what I can," Slocum said, coming to a conclusion. Pauline blinked as he walked by her. He paused for a moment, wondering if her husband and Grimsby might have circled around to join some unknown tracker he knew was behind them on their trail. Slocum decided it wasn't likely. He thought he heard the two men arguing, their voices carrying on the brisk wind whipping along the mountainside.

He left the trail and worked his way down a barren gully cut by melting snow and the incessant wind. A few black-furred marmots chittered angrily at him for disturbing their serene home, but he saw no trace of other game. Even rabbits found it difficult living at this altitude, with its bitter cold and short growing season. Slocum slipped and slid down a steep incline and lay on his belly, listening hard.

He heard a horse neighing and knew he was close to the man pursuing them. Slocum found scant vegetation for cover. The man on their tail had stopped in a stand of wind-blown junipers, just below the timberline. As far as his campsite went, the man had better sense than Yoakum. The low shrubs growing higher up the mountain afforded far less protection to the tourists camping for the night.

Slocum sat and waited for any hint as to the man after them. He thought he heard horse's hooves clacking on stone. If so, the man was retreating down the winding trail. After spending a few minutes more, Slocum knew his vigil would be unavailing. He got back to the trail and hiked up to where Pauline tried to show two of the men how to fasten the canvas to make a lean-to.

Yoakum and Hector Grimsby still hadn't returned, and it was starting to get dark. On the eastern slope of steep

Pikes Peak, daylight hours were shorter than expected by the Denver tourists. Slocum did what he could to help them get shelter against the icy wind, then hunted for a place to settle down himself after Pauline served dinner.

The few camp fires died when the men didn't get up to throw new wood on them. Slocum didn't much blame them for letting the fires die. Wood was scarce at the timberline, and except for dried burro dung from earlier treks to the summit, only a few twisted shrubs promised any hope of fuel. He pulled his blanket closer around his shoulders and tried to find a comfortable spot among the rocks.

"John," whispered the wind. "John?"

He sat up abruptly, hand on his Colt. A dark figure knelt a few feet away.

"Pauline?" He looked around and saw that the tourists had fallen into fitful sleep. The wind gusted occasionally, making the canvas flap loudly. But it had been the woman who called his name, not the night wind.

"I couldn't sleep," she said, but Slocum read more into her words. He silently reached out for her, and she melted into his arms, snuggling down. She trembled, and he wasn't sure if it was from the cold.

But she was another man's wife. Still, there couldn't be anything wrong in holding her. It felt right to Slocum. She cried a little and then went to sleep with her head resting on his shoulder.

Slocum lay on his back, staring at the clouds moving so quickly past the stars, obscuring them for a few seconds or minutes and then boldly revealing their blazing glory. There was so much he didn't know. Charley Yoakum. Hector Grimsby and their robbery. And Pauline. He didn't know what he would do.

Cutting down Charley Yoakum was something he would enjoy, but what would Pauline think of him if he did? She was married to the man and was unhappy, but Slocum had seen viewpoints change dramatically. Killing her husband might do that, even if he had beat her up and made her miserable. Slocum just didn't know the answers.

He lay back and stared at the sky, as if the answers were there. And then he slipped into fitful sleep, liking Pauline's body close to him and knowing he shouldn't.

15

Slocum came awake with a start, thinking Pauline had stirred enough to disturb him. But she still lay with her head cradled on his shoulder. The wind had risen but not enough to worry about a summer storm. Icy cold settled on the eastern slope of Pikes Peak—and in Slocum's stomach. Not ten feet away he saw a shadow moving toward him.

He shrugged and got Pauline off him. She mumbled in her sleep but did not awaken. Slocum pulled his Colt Navy and rolled away, finding a depression to lie in if he had to draw fire away from the woman. If one of the tourists had been stirring, they wouldn't have come on cat's feet like this stealthy visitor.

Cocking his six-shooter, Slocum waited to see what he had to do. The dark figure loomed near Pauline. Slocum didn't like using her as bait, but that seemed to be what he was doing. Just as he started to call out and draw attention away from her, the formless shape reached out and grabbed her shoulder.

Pauline yelped, and a hand muffled her cries.

"Dammit, woman, don't go cryin' out," came Charley Yoakum's voice.

"Wh-what do you want, Charley?" Pauline fought to clear the sleep from her eyes and brain. She struggled to sit up, but her husband shoved her back harshly. Slocum heard her head hit a rock with a dull crunch. Pauline moaned but said nothing about it. This was the treatment she had come to expect at her husband's hand.

"You know damn well what I want. Where's that drifter? The one riding with the tourists?"

"Mr. Slocum?" Real fear entered her voice now. Slocum didn't have to see Pauline's face to know how frightened she was of her husband.

"Who the hell else? Grimsby thinks he's a lawman, but I ain't so sure. Who is he and why's he here?"

"I thought he was just another sightseer from Denver."

Yoakum hit her. Slocum's finger almost drew back on the trigger.

"Don't lie. You ain't good at it. Never were. I got to know who he is or I'll have to kill him. And you, if you and him been doin' anything you shouldn't."

"Charley, please. I don't know anything about him. I just met him in . . . Manitou Springs." Pauline didn't lie well, but it was enough to keep her husband from hitting her again.

"You better not be lyin', bitch. There's more ridin' on this than you might think." Yoakum faded back into the darkness without another word. Slocum saw him go and considered what he might do.

He crawled back to Pauline, who jumped in fright at his sudden reappearance.

"John, my husband just—"

"I know. Go on back to sleep. I'll take care of this."

Her eyes widened when she saw the pistol in his hand. Pauline shook her head and tried to speak. Slocum silenced her in the only way he could. He kissed her.

"I'll be back. Don't worry about anything." Slocum left before she could get her wits about her and protest enough to make him stay.

He quickly left her behind, moving like a ghost across the rugged face of Pikes Peak. The wind blowing over the patches of snow chilled him, but inside a fire of outrage burned. Yoakum had no call treating Pauline the way he did. She knew nothing of Slocum's business. If Yoakum wanted to know, he should have broached Slocum about it instead of hitting his wife.

Yoakum had gone downhill, toward the timberline. Slocum found the going rough, but Yoakum knew the terrain well, judging from the ease with which he crossed it. Falling farther behind because of his trouble getting over rocky patches that cut and tore at his legs, Slocum had to content himself with keeping Yoakum in sight rather than overtaking him. Besides, Slocum was curious where the man had run off to so fast. Yoakum had the appearance of a man on a mission, intent on getting somewhere in a hurry.

Stumbling and trying not to make much noise, Slocum trailed him at a slower pace, reaching the timberline long minutes after Yoakum had entered the sparsely wooded area.

He had no trouble finding Yoakum, though, in the pitch-dark forest. The man's grating voice carried well enough for Slocum to home in on it like a bee finding a flower. Slocum dropped behind a fallen tree and peered over the edge into a small clearing where Yoakum paced angrily. As he walked to and fro, he berated his companion for being a fool. Slocum didn't have to see the second man to know who it was.

"Dammit, Grimsby," Yoakum finally said, "you were supposed to fetch the equipment we'd need. Is this it?" Yoakum kicked at a pile of rope.

"That's all I could find. What did you want, ladders?"

Yoakum's answer surprised Slocum.

"Yeah, that's exactly what we need. What am I supposed to do with this rotted rope? Swing like some damned monkey?"

Slocum thought Yoakum might swing one day, but it wouldn't be like a monkey. Slocum touched the butt of his six-shooter and knew he would save the law the effort of bringing Yoakum to trial and sentencing him to hang. But what did Yoakum want with a ladder on the side of Pikes Peak?

"We can't get back down the trail in time," Yoakum went on. "That means those tenderfeet will have to get on up to the top. We'll do it there."

"I don't know, Charley," Grimsby said, obviously unhappy with some aspect of their enigmatic scheme. "I want to go through with this, but I've never done anything like it before."

"If you can rob your own damned stores, you can do this. There's no difference." Yoakum's contempt was lost on Hector Grimsby.

"That's only money. It's different," Grimsby insisted. Slocum didn't have a clue what the men were arguing over, but it didn't sound as if the telegram he sought was involved. With three-quarters of the information needed, he wasn't going to give up trying to find who had received the telegram. If it wasn't Charley Yoakum, it had to be someone else at the Lake House.

"Let's ride," Yoakum said. "We're wasting time." He kicked at the pile of rope contemptuously.

"I got the horses, just like you said. They're tethered back there." Grimsby pointed to a dark patch of forest. Slocum strained and heard the faint sounds of horses. He began moving to get a better view of what the hardware magnate had assembled in the way of horseflesh. Reaching the area before Grimsby and Yoakum, Slocum was startled to see six horses.

He ducked behind a tree as Yoakum swung into sight, swaggering now.

"This is better," Yoakum said, seeing the horses. "We'll need two for pack, and the others we can ride."

"There's no need to go on and do this, Charley," complained Grimsby. Whatever conspiracy drove them, Grimsby was backing out. Slocum almost chuckled at that. The man talked as big as his waist, but when it came to doing, Hector

Grimsby was a failure. That might explain why he couldn't keep his wife in line.

"Why not? After we exchange favors, we're gonna need some money. This is the best way of getting it."

"I've got plenty," Grimsby said uneasily. The corpulent man shifted about, staring at the horses as if they might rear up and stomp him into the ground at any instant. From the set to Charley Yoakum's shoulders, the only thing Grimsby had to fear was his partner's wrath.

"*You've* got the money. I don't, but I will after this." Yoakum saddled a horse and took the reins of another. "I'll take the gear down lower and cache it near the Lake House. When we get the other chores done, then we can use it. And I got one final thing to tend to before we get down to business tomorrow." Yoakum rode into the dark, heading downhill to the path they had traversed. On a horse, riding at a decent pace, Slocum knew Yoakum could get to the hotel and back before morning. He might be able to make it in an hour or two, instead of the day-long trip required because of the tourists and their sightseeing.

Hector Grimsby shifted uneasily, as if not sure what he was supposed to do. He finally left the remaining horses and walked off into the night, blundering around like a drunken bull. Slocum had no trouble following the portly man's progress.

He was so engrossed in tracking Grimsby he didn't hear a bushwhacker come up behind him. The first hint Slocum had that he had been found was the bullet ripping through his side. White-hot pain blasted into his left side and doubled him up. This reflex action to the injury saved his life. Slocum's head dropped enough that a second bullet missed, sending chips from a tree trunk flying in all directions.

Slocum crumpled to the ground, clutching his side. He forced himself to lift his six-shooter, but he had no target. All he knew was that the man drygulching him was somewhere behind, in the trees.

A third shot rang out and almost ended Slocum's life, but this time he was ready. He jerked to the left and fell flat on the ground as a bright flash from the gun's muzzle showed. Having a target now, Slocum began firing, slowly, deliberately. He thought he might have winged his attacker, but he couldn't be sure.

Ears ringing from the gunshots, Slocum tried to hear where his assailant moved. He couldn't. Slocum's fingers probed his left side, causing new waves of pain to rock his senses. He didn't think the bullet had done any real damage, but his fingers came away sticky with blood. It might have been one of those wounds that looked—and felt—worse than it really was. Only careful examination would tell.

If Slocum got the chance.

A new hail of bullets kicked up the forest around him, sending pine needles and dirt flying. He didn't stay prone, because this only provided a target for his unseen bush-whacker. Getting to his feet, Slocum swung around a tree, feinted left, and ran for all his worth to the right. He tried to keep track of where the horses were, where Grimsby might have gone, and how to get back to where the tourists camped.

Slocum didn't want to return straightaway, though, without dealing with his attacker. He wanted to know who this back-shooter was—and stop him dead.

His resolve flagged a mite when he had to dodge four more rounds. He had misjudged where his attacker was. He sucked in a deep breath and felt the air rattle through his tortured lungs. His side burned as if a million ants had taken up residence in his chest. Slocum tried to remember how many times he had fired and couldn't.

Two? Three, he decided. That didn't leave him much leeway to fight. Better to return to camp and find some safety in numbers. He didn't think any of the men in the group had a six-shooter, and he knew none had a rifle, but whoever had tried to shoot him couldn't kill everyone.

Slocum found the edge of the wooded area and stared at the barren area leading to the ravine he had followed to reach this spot. The ankle-high grass gave no cover to anyone ducking a sniper in the woods. Slocum waited for a heavy cloud to come scudding over, obscuring the bright stars, before making a break.

The first bullet knocked Slocum's foot from under him, sending him rolling. He smashed hard into a rock. The wave of pain passing over him threatened to drown him. His side exploded in a Fourth of July display of suffering that threatened to make him pass out. Slocum grunted as a new round came close to killing him.

He forced his hand to hoist his six-shooter and fire. He shot in the direction of the unseen sniper, but Slocum had no hope of hitting anyone. The recoil almost knocked the pistol from his weakening hand. Slocum shook himself, trying to concentrate on the pain in his side to keep himself alert. Any inattention now spelled his death at the hands of the hidden gunman.

Slocum's hammer fell on an empty cylinder. He tried to keep firing, as if he would somehow find a round miraculously loaded. Two new bullets dug into the hard dirt at his feet as the sniper homed in on him.

Slocum rolled over and lay flat in a shallow depression, still twenty feet from the deeper ravine that might let him get back to camp alive.

As he lay facedown, he noticed a hard spot in his vest pocket. His brother Robert's watch was on the other side. Slocum moved around and touched the derringer he had tucked there after his ineffectual duel with Hector Grimsby. The vest was the only item he'd kept.

Slocum drew the tiny pistol and waited, thinking he would have one shot if the bushwhacker came over to make sure of his kill. More rounds sang through the windy night, causing rock and dirt to dance just above Slocum's head. Any chance of reaching the ravine evaporated now. The drygulching son of a bitch had his range now.

Slocum waited, expecting a bullet to take him at any instant. But a new sound came to him, a rifle report. He thought the gunman had changed weapons, then he heard the higher pitched sound of a firing six-gun. The sniper exchanged fire with someone else, someone using a rifle.

The gunfire continued for almost a minute, then stopped. The silence rang like thunder in Slocum's ears. He lay flat, gripping the derringer tightly until his hand cramped. There was no way to tell who had won the brief but fierce gunfight that had so unexpectedly erupted. Someone had come to his rescue, but had they prevailed?

Slocum didn't know. All he could do was wait. After ten minutes of listening to his own beating heart, Slocum poked his head up and looked around. Dizziness hit him like a sledgehammer blow. Wobbling, he put his forehead against the rocky side of the narrow gully, where he lay until the dizziness passed.

He saw no trace of either gunman or rescuer. He knew from the way his knees had turned to rubber that he required bandaging. His side throbbed mercilessly from the first round he had taken. His foot twitched and jerked, but the slug that had gone through his boot hadn't hit anything important. He could walk. Barely.

Stumbling, forcing himself to keep going in spite of the pain in his side, Slocum made his way to the deeper ravine leading uphill to the tourists' camp. He was safe, or as safe as he could get for the moment. Someone had brought him deliverance, but who was it? He had seen Charley Yoakum ride off, heading downhill toward the Lake House. If he assumed that the bushwhacker was the same man who had killed Andrew and his girlfriend back in Manitou Springs, that left only Hector Grimsby as his savior.

Or was Grimsby the attacker and someone else his rescuer? As he plodded along, Slocum tried to sort it all out and found that he couldn't. Too many people wanted him dead, and he didn't know who they were—or why.

16

He was being fired on from all directions. Quantrill had lied to them before the raid. There was opposition. Lots of it. The Missouri farmers had taken up arms to fire at any rebel guerrilla they saw riding across their land. Slocum ducked and dodged, trying to find just the right escape through the intense fire. He twisted about violently and hit the ground hard when a bullet caught him on the top of his head.

But the wound turned from blood to water. He tasted the sweet, cool water on his lips, running down his throat. Stirring, he tried to see how this was possible. He had to escape the deadly fire mowing them down. Quantrill had lied. Their smiling, confident, cold-blooded leader had made a mistake.

"It's all right, John. Don't fight. You're running a little fever, but I don't think it is too serious." A cool hand pressed against his forehead. More water trickled across his parched lips.

"Gotta get away. Can't let 'em shoot us like that."

"Who shot you?" The voice was familiar. It wasn't Quantrill. It certainly wasn't Bill Anderson. He always rode into battle like some ancient berserker, frothing at the mouth like a mad dog and shouting at the top of his lungs.

Slocum forced himself to remain calm. To his surprise, he discovered that his eyes were screwed tightly shut. He relaxed enough to open them. Confusion seized him for a moment. He wasn't in Missouri. Or even Kansas. He tried to figure out how he had been transported across space like this in the twinkling of an eye.

"Shot," he got out, turning to see who tended him. An angel bent closer, and Slocum knew he was bound for heaven—or hell. She brushed his face with a tumble of dark hair, then kissed him.

That kiss brought a semblance of sanity back to him. He wasn't still fighting the war. And this wasn't Missouri.

"Pikes Peak," he got out. "I was following Yoakum and got shot." The memory flooding back on him was almost as painful as his fever dream of slaughtering any man in his path who might harbor Yankee sympathies. He had made a mistake, and it had almost gotten him killed.

"I heard the gunfire about the time Charley rode into camp. He refused to go see what was happening. Said it was a hunter, though no one hunts at four in the morning," Pauline said. Slocum remembered her name and how he had come to be here. He tried sitting up, but the world refused to stop spinning long enough for him to make it.

Pauline squeezed more water from a rag onto his lips. She reached out and dabbed at his forehead. The pain in his side had subsided from a raging forest fire to a smoldering pit that scorched brain and body. But it was bearable.

"I did the best I could. It seems all I do is patch you up, John."

"I'll try not to get shot again," he promised her. The next time it would be his unseen bushwhacker who would pay. His green eyes focused on Pauline, and he asked, "You said Yoakum was here? With you?"

Pauline nodded. "He rode into camp about five minutes before the shooting started. He was furious with me and demanded that I give him the telegram my brother sent."

"What?" Slocum's head spun again.

"I didn't understand what the rush was. My brother sent me a telegram, and Charley came riding in demanding to see it. Well, he demanded to see all the telegrams, but I had only the one Matt sent."

"Matt Burnside?"

"Why, yes. How'd you know, John?" Pauline frowned, then sat back. "I don't understand any of this. Charley took it, but I don't know why. He's never met my brother, and I certainly never told Matt about Charley." Pauline looked chagrined. "I never told any of my family about him." She snorted ruefully. "I never even told them I was getting married."

"A number," Slocum said. "That's all there was in it, right?"

"How *do* you know that? Did you read it? Do you know Matt? Why'd Charley want it? And who's shooting at you? What's going on, John? Tell me." Pauline alternated between being frightened and furious at the way she was being treated. Slocum had even worse news for her.

"Your brother's dead," he said. There wasn't any reason to add sugar to sweeten the news. "He got killed during a bank robbery in Denver."

"Dead?" Pauline fought to hold back the tears but couldn't.

"He took the gold, and I want to find it. The telegram he sent to PB told where it is." More to settle it in his own mind, Slocum softly added, "Pauline Burnside." That much made sense now. It had been in front of him, and he hadn't asked the one person who could to help him.

"How can that number tell you anything?"

"Your husband took the telegram." Slocum cursed himself anew for asking Charley Yoakum about the telegram. He had set the man to thinking. Yoakum might not know how to use the number in the telegram, but he could keep Slocum from recovering the gold. One, two, or three clues meant nothing without the fourth.

The one riding in Yoakum's pocket.

"Don't sound so despondent," Pauline said, dabbing at her tears. "You haven't lost a brother. Oh, I knew he was mixed up with something illegal. Matt always had more money than he could have made being a telegrapher."

"I know how it feels. I've lost a brother," Slocum said softly. He sat up and fought against the dizziness. He took Pauline in his arms. Somehow, it felt right. He wasn't sure if it helped her grief any, but it helped him. He might have lost the gold, but this was some consolation.

Some.

"Where's your husband?" he asked after Pauline's grief had subsided a mite. "I might still get the telegram back from him."

"He rode off. I don't know where. I got the impression he was heading back to the Lake House."

Slocum thought for a moment. On their way up Pikes Peak, the tourists traveled light, leaving most of their belongings at the hotel for their return from the grand adventure. He suspected they would find their rooms rifled and anything of value stolen. And Charley Yoakum would be responsible.

Yoakum and Hector Grimsby. That started Slocum thinking in different directions. If Yoakum hadn't fired on him, being as he was in camp stealing Pauline's telegram, that meant Grimsby had either tried to kill him or rescue him. But which was it? And who was the third man?

Slocum's head and side began hurting too much for him to continue.

"This will work out," Slocum told Pauline. "We'll take your tourists back to the hotel in a couple hours and—"

"No!" Pauline turned adamant. "I'll see them to the summit. They paid their money. If you're not up to the ride, you can stay here and we'll pick you up on the way back."

"Your husband's probably robbing their rooms right now," Slocum told her.

Pauline shook her head. "All the more reason to take them to the top. Give them one pleasant memory. Either way, when they return, this will ruin the Lake House's reputation. There's no way we can stop him from burgling their rooms now, is there?"

"None," Slocum agreed. He wasn't up to fighting the man. He wanted to get his strength back—and reload his Colt Navy. The single shot he carried in the derringer wouldn't be enough when he faced down Charley Yoakum.

"So, it's decided," Pauline said, as if a weight had been lifted.

"Pauline," he said slowly, "what would you do if you came into a lot of money?"

"Divorce Charley," she said without hesitation. "I've asked a lawyer in Denver about it. It will cost almost fifty dollars. It might as well be fifty thousand because Charley takes every penny I earn. I've tried to put away a little, but he always finds it."

"If I find him, you won't need a divorce. You'll be a widow," Slocum said, hoping she wouldn't think too poorly of him for the admission.

Pauline nodded. "I thought as much. Somehow, that's not much of a shock to me, not as much as finding out Matt is dead."

"What will you do? Once you're free of Yoakum?" Slocum wasn't sure what he was asking. And neither was Pauline.

"There won't be a job for me at the hotel. Maybe I can find something in the Springs. Or even in Denver. I know people." She smiled almost shyly. "The engineer and conductor on General Palmer's train like me. I might even get a job with the D&RG." She laughed without humor. "Matt had even shown me how to use a key. Maybe I can practice and learn telegraphy."

She paused and looked hard at him before asking, "If you find out what's in the wire Matt sent, what then?"

"I'm rich," Slocum said simply. "We'd be rich."

"You'd share with me? Why?"

They stared into each other's eyes, then turned away, as embarrassed as if they were schoolchildren considering a first kiss.

"You're due Matt's share, no matter what. That's only fair. But I'd want you to have a stake in the rest, too. I reckon I'm the only one left to claim it."

"It's not yours. You said you stole it."

"We did," Slocum said. "Does that matter?"

"I don't know," she said simply, wrestling with a difficult moral decision, but Slocum knew everything would work out. He'd find Yoakum and pry the telegram from the man's dead fingers. He took Pauline in his arms again and just held her. It felt right. Damned right.

She gently pushed him back to the blanket, slid under with him, and they lay side by side until the sun began turning the distant eastern horizon pink with dawn.

Slocum didn't ride any better than the greenhorns, but he didn't ride much worse, either. He was weak from loss of blood, and more than once the pain made him woozy, but he rode alongside Pauline without falling off his surefooted burro. She had taken charge of the group with a skill Slocum appreciated.

He had watched her go about the chore of rounding up her charges, getting them fed with a simple but filling breakfast, and starting for the top of the mountain. But Slocum was aggravated that Hector Grimsby was nowhere to be seen. His wife didn't seem worried at his disappearance, nor could Adeline Grimsby explain it.

"He's always going off like this," the annoying woman assured Slocum. "It has its advantages, you realize." She batted her long black eyelashes in his direction, but Slocum wanted none of what she so blatantly offered. He had excused himself to help Pauline, much to Adeline Grimsby's irritation.

Had Hector Grimsby been his savior or attacker? Slocum wouldn't know until he faced the portly man and looked him square in the eye. Grimsby wasn't much of a liar. For all that, he wasn't much of a man.

"There it is!" shouted Pauline, pointing ahead along the steep trail. "Pikes Peak. We've reached the summit!"

The burros kept moving at their slow pace, but a shiver of excitement passed through the group. To Slocum it was just another mountaintop. He had trouble breathing because of the height, and his side burned with renewed fire. But the sight was nothing he hadn't experienced a dozen times from a dozen other tall mountains. Pikes Peak wasn't even the highest in Colorado, not by thirty other names.

"There's Denver," someone chirped rushing toward the easternmost side of the broad mountaintop. "And there, there's Colorado City. And . . ." The tourists dismounted and scattered across Pikes Peak's rounded summit.

Slocum slipped off the burro, settled himself until the pain abated, and went to help Pauline take out fixings for a lunch. He hoped the trip back down the mountain went quicker than the journey up. He figured it might, now that the men and women had reached their goal. They would be in a hurry to return to the Lake House and the fashionable party promised them.

He chuckled at the reception they would receive. There might be a lavish party, but they would also find their rooms cleaned out by Charley Yoakum and Hector Grimsby. Slocum frowned as that thought crossed his mind. Yoakum's petty thievery he understood. But why had Hector Grimsby joined him? Because he hadn't killed Slocum? That was the only explanation, though the man might have bluffed his way clear if he had faced down Slocum. Slocum had not seen his ambusher. And if Grimsby had been doing any shooting from the shadows, he could have claimed to be Slocum's rescuer.

"The wicked flee when no man pursueth," Slocum quoted from Proverbs. He settled down on his haunches and stared into the distance. He might not be righteous, but he was certainly bold. And when he and Pauline got back to Denver, they would be rich. Finding the Denver and Rio Grande freight car carrying the number riding in Pauline's telegram would be easy. Searching for the hidden compartment would be even simpler. He and Pauline would be rich.

All he had to do was track down Yoakum and take the telegram.

"There you are, John," came Adeline Grimsby's voice. Slocum saw the woman bustling over to him, determination burning in her eyes. He couldn't simply take off running, though he wanted to. "You've been avoiding me. There's no need. I don't bite." She batted her eyelashes again and said in a husky whisper she probably thought was sexy, "Unless you want me to."

"Mrs. Grimsby, I've got work to do. I promised Mrs. Yoakum that—"

"You do too much for someone who ought to be enjoying himself. Who ought to be enjoying what life has to offer." Again sotto voce she added, "What I have to offer." She puffed up her chest to its ample proportions and clung to his arm with a tenacity Slocum had found only in southern swamp leeches.

Adeline Grimsby almost dragged him away from the others, going toward the southern slope of Pikes Peak. Huge rock ridges rose, cutting them off from sight. Slocum tried to steer her to the north, where most of the tourists had gone. From there he could see taller Colorado mountains, Mt. Elbert and Mt. Massive, but Adeline Grimsby wasn't interested in sightseeing.

She pulled him toward the edge of a long drop, turned, and began unfastening the buttons on her blouse. "This is what you want to see, isn't it, John?"

Slocum backed off a step and started to speak. Anything he might have said was drowned by the single shot that rang out. Adeline Grimsby looked startled. Her mouth opened and closed, and then she fell backward, tumbling over the ledge.

A jumble of thoughts flashed through Slocum's head. He grabbed for his Colt Navy, drew, and whipped around, only to find that Charley Yoakum had the drop on him. White smoke from the muzzle of the man's six-shooter curled up to be caught on the brisk wind whipping over the summit.

"Drop your hogleg, Slocum," came the cold command. Slocum saw no hint of tremor in Yoakum's grip. If he didn't obey, he'd be shot as Adeline Grimsby had been. Slocum dropped his six-gun to the ground.

"Why'd you shoot her?"

Yoakum laughed harshly. "I'm a damned good shot," Yoakum bragged. "It wasn't because I missed you. I *wanted* her hoppin' over the coals in hell."

"Grimsby," Slocum said, a piece of the puzzle sliding into place. "He hired you to kill his wife."

"Hired? He doesn't have enough money. We're partners, for the time bein'." Yoakum moved around to the edge of the cliff and looked over. A broad grin spread across his face. "She's good 'n dead. Just the way I intended."

"Grimsby's at the Lake House robbing the rooms," Slocum guessed. He had been wrong last night. Yoakum had come back to Pauline to take the telegram while Grimsby had gone back downhill to the hotel. Slocum thought Hector Grimsby might have seen him, done some shooting, and then hightailed it to the Lake House.

But who had come to his rescue? The bushwhacker had used a six-shooter, and the second gunman had fired a rifle. The reports were unmistakable to Slocum's experienced ear.

He pushed that from his mind. He had other, more immediate problems. He looked from the bore of Yoakum's six-shooter to the Colt Navy on the ground. If Yoakum intended killing him, he had nothing to lose going for his six-shooter.

"Yeah, if he don't screw that up, too. He hasn't got much right yet," said Yoakum.

"Why didn't you cut me down with her?" Slocum jerked his thumb in Adeline Grimsby's direction. He hoped Yoakum would glance back, giving him the chance to dive for his gun. Yoakum's cold, flinty eyes never left Slocum.

"I got a question for you." Yoakum reached into his shirt pocket and pulled out a telegram. The telegram. It flapped loudly in the rising wind. "What's this here number mean? You been nosing around like a bear huntin' for a honeycomb. Pauline said she don't know what this means, but she's one lyin' bitch. But *you* know."

Slocum's eyes fixed on the flimsy yellow paper. He'd go to his death before he told Charley Yoakum what it meant.

Slocum's eyes went toward the south, over the brink of the mountain. His shoulders shifted as if he were going to dive over. He twisted, ducked, and dove, scrabbling for his six-shooter. His feint worked to get Yoakum's line of fire off-center. The bullet sang past Slocum and into empty space.

His hand closed around the ebony handle of his Colt. Slocum rolled over and fired. The hammer fell on an empty chamber. The six-shooter hadn't been reloaded.

Yoakum shifted slightly and widened his stance. "You're dead, Slocum. You ought to have checked your piece."

Yoakum lifted his six-shooter and aimed, the sights square on the middle of Slocum's forehead.

The shot ringing out was dull, hollow, almost comical in its pygmy report. But Yoakum stiffened and reached for the spot where the derringer round had entered his chest. Slocum had succeeded in getting the two-barreled pistol free from his vest pocket in time to fire.

"No!" Slocum shouted as Yoakum dropped his gun—and the telegram slipped from between his dead fingers. Charley Yoakum toppled over the edge of the cliff, following Adeline Grimsby.

And Matt Burnside's telegram fluttered away, caught on the wind, sailing far out of Slocum's reach.

17

Slocum watched as the yellow paper fluttered far away, out of reach. It eventually vanished against the brilliant blue Colorado sky. He sagged a little, having come so close to being rich. The secret hiding place of the gold would never be known now. He had no intention of going through every D&RG freight car hunting for a secret hiding place. That would be both dangerous and downright foolish.

Matt Burnside wouldn't have put the gold somewhere it would be easily found.

Slocum edged closer and stared over the edge of Pikes Peak. Adeline Grimsby's body lay in a crumpled mass a hundred feet below. Of Yoakum's body he saw nothing. The man had taken quite a step backward when the slug from Slocum's derringer caught him squarely in the center of his chest.

"Rich or alive," sighed Slocum. What a choice. But he knew it was better to be rid of Charley Yoakum than to be rich. The telegram was gone, and he wasn't the kind to cry over spilled milk. But he had another problem to face. For all of Pauline's contention that she wanted to be free of her husband, Slocum wasn't sure how she would take it knowing he was dead. And that Slocum was the one who'd plugged the worthless bastard.

Slocum picked up his Colt Navy and tucked it into his cross-draw holster. He had to reload to be ready for such showdowns. Only the bullet wound in his side had distracted him this time—and it had almost meant his life. He balanced the derringer in his hand for a moment, then cast it over the side, after Yoakum and Adeline Grimsby. He had no further need for it.

Hiking back to the burros took away his wind. He sank down to rest when Pauline came over.

"I wondered where you had gone. You and Adeline Grimsby," she said accusingly.

"You don't need to look for her," Slocum said, wondering how to tell Pauline her husband was dead, too. He had come right out with the news of her brother's death. He didn't want the woman to think of him as the one who always brought bad news.

"What happened, John?" Pauline looked over her shoulder. The other tourists continued their frolicking about at the top of the world, oblivious to the twin deaths that had occurred not fifty yards from them.

"Your husband. Charley shot her."

"Shot her?" exclaimed Pauline. She fought to keep down her voice. "Why? He's crazy as a bedbug, but he had no call to kill her."

"He did," Slocum said, suddenly worried and not knowing why. He was missing something and didn't know what it might be. "And you won't have to worry about getting a divorce from him. He won't be coming back to bother you again."

The grimness in his voice told Pauline everything she needed to know. A tiny trapped animal sound left her mouth, then she sat heavily and stared into the distance. She stared and didn't see. Slocum let her be with her thoughts for a spell before saying anything more.

"He murdered her and would have killed me, too. It was self-defense."

"I know, John. You're not the kind to shoot people in

the back. But this is such a blow. Matt, Charley. Everyone I know is dying."

Slocum started to mention how Yoakum had taken the telegram with him, but he thought better of it. Pauline was suffering, and the telegram meant less to her than it did to him. She was the one who had lost two members of her family, even if Charley Yoakum hadn't been worthy of being kin to such a fine woman.

"They're about ready to return," Pauline said in a choked voice. "We can get back to the hotel by late afternoon. It's all downhill from here." She laughed harshly at this. "All downhill."

"I'll see to the burros," Slocum volunteered. "I don't think any of them will even notice Adeline Grimsby isn't with us."

Pauline shrugged. "No one mentioned Hector Grimsby's absence this morning. If anything, they might wonder why it is so quiet. I declare, that woman never shut up. Her jaw flapped constantly."

Slocum touched Pauline on the arm. She smiled wanly and quickly left. Slocum didn't press the point. He had no idea how she felt. For all Pauline knew, he might have killed her brother, too.

He got to work with the burros, getting them ready for the trip back to the Lake House. Slocum smiled without humor at the thought of Hector Grimsby going through the tourists' rooms, stealing anything of value. What would the portly man do when his partner never joined him?

Again, some small detail nagged at the edges of Slocum's mind, but the returning sightseers made him lose track of his thought. He greeted them, helped two of the women onto their burros, and generally complimented them on their good taste in choosing to be led to Pikes Peak by the staff at the Lake House. For this he received a genuine smile from Pauline, that quickly faded as memories returned.

Slocum led the string of burros back to the edge of the mountain and down the winding path. He wanted to ride beside Pauline, but she brought up the rear, as if this were the only place for her. Slocum set a fast pace, but the tourists were tired of the scenery by now and no one complained too much. It was late afternoon when he slid off his burro and helped the others from their saddles.

"I'll get the animals into the corral," Slocum told Pauline. "You see to your guests."

"All right, John," she said. She started to say something more, then fell silent. Her dark eyes fixed squarely on him, as if more than words welled up inside but wouldn't come. "We'll talk later."

He nodded. Tending the burros would be easier than anything the woman might have to say to him. She'd had all day to blame him for her husband's death—and maybe her brother's, as well. How Pauline would explain Adeline Grimsby's absence to the manager and his wife, Slocum didn't know. She might not even mention it. Explaining away her own husband's disappearance might be harder, since Charley Yoakum worked for the hotel.

Having finished with the burros, certain that they had ample feed and water, Slocum walked slowly toward the Lake House. As he neared the structure, the thought that had been nagging him all day came back.

"Grimsby." Slocum turned in a full circle and decided the man was most likely to use Yoakum's encampment a few hundred yards from the hotel. He drew his Colt Navy and checked the cylinder, making sure it carried six loads. He had forgotten to reload once. He wouldn't a second time.

Slocum found Yoakum's small campsite and five horses tethered there. He wondered where Yoakum had left the horse he had ridden to the summit of Pikes Peak, then pushed such thoughts aside. The horse would manage on its own. One of these horses had been rigged as a pack animal, two saddled for riding, and the remaining two left as spares for a quick ride away. Slocum wasn't sure where the men had intended going. Around Mystic Lake, across Ruxton Park, south, north—there was no telling. They might even have considered going downhill to Manitou Springs and out to Colorado City.

But the horses stood alone, and there wasn't any sign of Hector Grimsby. Slocum ran back to the hotel, his dread growing. If Yoakum had killed Adeline Grimsby, a deal might have been struck where Hector Grimsby was to kill Pauline. That would give Yoakum a hold over the portly man and keep him from backing out later. Grimsby would never go to the authorities if it meant a noose around his own fat neck.

And it would remove what Yoakum considered a thorn in his side: Pauline.

Twilight sent shadows skimming across the grass. In the main dining room, the tourists were gathered and gaily joking, bragging about their conquest of the high mountain and otherwise enjoying themselves. Grimsby must not have raided their rooms yet—and Pauline might still be safe.

The notion of Hector Grimsby swinging from ropes to enter the windows of the second-story rooms struck Slocum as ludicrous, yet the man had brought the gear. The need for ladders now fit nicely into the scheme Slocum realised Grimsby and Yoakum had concocted.

Slocum skidded to a halt when he saw a tall ladder leaning against the side of the hotel. The window to a room on the second floor had been pushed open, and Slocum thought he saw movement inside. He climbed the ladder quickly, poked his head over the windowsill, and dared a peek into the room. He didn't want to get his head blown off if Grimsby got buck fever and shot at anything moving.

The room was empty, but it had been ransacked. Slocum slid over the sill and dropped into the room. He drew his six-shooter and went to the door, peering into the hallway. A huge bag stuffed with the tourists' property sat in the middle of the narrow corridor. From two rooms down came a huffing and puffing, and Slocum knew he had found Hector Grimsby.

Closing the door until only a crack showed, Slocum

watched as Grimsby dumped jewelry and other belongings into the large bag. How the man intended to get such an ungainly parcel out was beyond Slocum, but Grimsby was a novice at this. He did his stealing from the cash till, overcharging a few dollars here and shortchanging there. He might even have staged a robbery or two of his own stores for insurance or to keep Adeline Grimsby from knowing he had squirreled away the money.

Slocum considered what to do, since Grimsby was still working so hard at his robbery. Getting the manager might be as easy a course as any. Then Slocum's options changed drastically. Pauline came up the stairs, and Hector Grimsby whirled about with surprising speed for a man as fat as he was. He yanked out a derringer, the twin to the one Slocum had thrown over the edge of Pikes Peak. He cocked the large-caliber, two-shot gun and shoved it into Pauline's face.

"Get in here. Now!" Grimsby's voice almost broke with strain. Pauline was speechless. She let him shove her into the room at the end of the hall.

Slocum threw open the door and started to fire, but he had missed his opportunity. Grimsby and Pauline were out of sight. Slocum hopped over the bag of stolen goods and grabbed the doorknob. Locked. He pressed his ear against the door panel and heard Grimsby's breathy voice.

"I don't want to do this, but Yoakum killed my wife. It's only fair that I settle accounts by killing you."

Slocum imagined the fat man's hand shaking uncontrollably. Killing a man in a drunken duel was different from murdering a woman in cold blood. Slocum stepped from the door, put his back against the wall, then kicked like a mule. The lock exploded from the doorjamb and the door slammed back.

In the split second before the door rebounded, Slocum's quick eyes took in the scene. Grimsby had the derringer leveled at Pauline. His finger tensed on the trigger until the knuckle turned white. He was going to fire.

Slocum got off a round that took Hector Grimsby in the side of the head. Then the rebounding door blocked Slocum's view. He drove forward again, using his shoulder on the unlocked door. He tumbled into the room and fired a second time.

It wasn't needed. Grimsby was already sagging to the floor, his sightless eyes staring only at death.

"Pauline, are you all right?" Slocum had seen more than one man get off a shot or more while dying. His bullet had ripped through Grimsby's temple and blown his brains out, but a dying spasm could have fired the derringer. It hadn't.

"John, I—" Pauline was pale and shaken. She stood to one side and just shook. He grabbed her and held her close.

"We've got to get out of here. Is there anything you want from your room?"

"Clothing. I need clothes."

"Never mind that," he said, thinking quickly. "I've got a few dollars. If we don't clear out before the hotel manager starts asking questions, we'll never be free."

"The bank robbery," she said. "You and Matt."

"And there will be questions about the Grimsbys and your husband I don't cotton much to answering." He didn't mention Andrew and his girlfriend back in Manitou Springs. And the Denver deputy whose brother had been killed in the robbery wouldn't take kindly to letting the murderer get away scot-free, either.

"We should stay and face the law, John. We haven't done anything. We're innocent!"

"You are. I'm not. Your brother and I robbed that bank. You can stay, if you want. I've got to go. And quick." Slocum heard footsteps coming up the stairs. Curiosity had overcome any fear the hotel manager might have had on hearing gunshots in his hotel.

"John, wait." Indecision crossed Pauline's face, then she made her decision. "I'll go with you."

"Come on." He tugged her toward the window. The ladder Hector Grimsby had leaned against the wall was too far away to be of any use. Slocum quickly lowered Pauline, holding her hands and then dropping her. He quickly followed, hitting the ground hard and rolling. Pain rippled through his side, but knowing the hell that would break loose when the hotel manager found Grimsby dead drove Slocum on.

He grabbed Pauline's hand again and dragged her toward her husband's campsite.

"Not so fast, John. I can't keep up."

"You have to. Grimsby and Yoakum had horses staked out for their getaway. We can take them and never slow down."

"Where are we going?" she asked.

"Anywhere, now that the telegram is lost," Slocum said. He, too, began to flag. The altitude took its toll on his endurance, and the pain in his side worsened with every step he took. "Your husband let it go when he went over the side on top of Pikes Peak."

"Why not go to Denver, if that's where the gold is?" asked Pauline.

"I don't know where the gold is," Slocum said bitterly. "I have three of the four clues your brother sent, but I need the final one. And it's lost."

"No, it isn't," Pauline said. Slocum skidded to a halt and spun around to face her.

"What do you mean?"

"Charley took the telegram, but I read it. It was only a number. That was why I was surprised when you said you knew what was in it."

"I knew it was a number but not what number," Slocum said.

"I read the telegram. I remember it. It was only a four-digit number." Pauline squealed when Slocum grabbed her and swung her around in a wide circle.

"You remember? You know the number? We're rich!"

His heart almost exploded in his chest. He had let a fortune slip through his fingers, and now it was his again!

"Of course, I do. Remember what you said up on the trail. I get a cut."

"You can have half of it," he said, spirit soaring. Things finally had gone his way. "We're the only ones left, except maybe for Slick Bob." He caught his breath and said, "We can't stay any longer. It's more important than ever to get to Denver. To the rail yard."

They burst into the small clearing where Charley Yoakum had camped and found the horses tethered where Grimsby had left them. Slocum ran straight for the animals, then slowed and finally stopped, staring at them.

"What's wrong, John?" Pauline asked.

Slocum didn't reply. There had been five horses here just a few minutes earlier. Now there were only four.

18

They rode far into the night and past that into morning, Slocum feeling, all the while that they were being trailed. He shook off the feeling, telling himself that the hotelier wasn't likely to come after them. Dana would be too busy trying to soothe the guests at the Lake House. Hector Grimsby's death wouldn't mean as much as the guests getting back their belongings. Grimsby hadn't been good enough a thief to get away with any of the jewelry or other valuables. None of the guests would care that he was dead.

But there would be a buzz when they couldn't find Adeline Grimsby. And someone would remember Charley Yoakum. And his wife. And maybe even Slocum. When the worry reached a certain level, the El Paso County sheriff would be contacted.

Slocum wanted to be in Denver when that happened. And if the sheriff wired Denver, Slocum wanted to have retrieved the gold from the bank robbery and be long gone. He turned grimmer thinking of the Denver deputy still on his trail. The man wasn't going to give up, and Slocum would have trouble asking after him. All he knew was the deputy's first name—Tom.

"You're mighty thoughtful, John," said Pauline. "We've

ridden so hard it's getting hard to sit in the saddle. Why don't we stop for a while and talk?"

Slocum wanted to push on. They could reach Denver in a couple days traveling hard. But he reined back. He owed Pauline a great deal.

"There's a cool-looking spot. Nice stream, shade."

"I'm hungry," complained Pauline.

"I'll shoot a rabbit for lunch," Slocum said. Pauline had wanted to linger in Manitou Springs and buy some vittles for the trip, but Slocum hadn't wanted to stay around for the stores to open. The entire town was a trap waiting to close around him. He rubbed his throat, imagining a hemp noose tightening there.

"All right," she said, "but there can't be that much hurry getting to Denver. You don't know if you'll be able to find the gold." Pauline's voice carried a sadness that told Slocum more than her words. She was returning to the city where her brother had died.

"We'll find it," Slocum said, his thoughts meandering. He didn't know what had happened to Slick Bob Durham. If Durham had ended up in jail, Slocum would have to get him out. But the gold came first. Use the number riding in Pauline's head to find the right D&RG freight car, *then* see to Slick Bob.

"I wish Matt hadn't gotten involved in a robbery," Pauline said. "He might still be alive."

Slocum said nothing in response to her daydream. Men like Matt Burnside found trouble if it didn't find them first. That was the way they lived. That was the way John Slocum lived.

After a noon meal, they pushed on and arrived in Denver. And the entire way, Slocum had an itchy feeling he couldn't shake.

"There's Matt's telegrapher's shack," Pauline said as they rode through the rail yards. Dozens of cars had been backed onto a siding near the Western Union building.

Slocum's quick eyes saw that none of these cars were D&RG freight cars.

"What's the number we're hunting for?" he asked.

"What does it match? A railway car?"

Pauline deserved to know that much. Slocum told her. Pauline nodded and said, "Three-one-two-three. That's all the telegram said."

"That's good enough. Where're the Denver and Rio Grande cars?" Slocum and Pauline searched for twenty minutes, and did not find any D&RG car matching that number.

"We can hunt forever, John," she told him. "Let me go talk to the dispatcher. He knows where every car is, both in the yard and along the lines."

"The dispatcher?" Slocum hadn't thought that the man shuttling trains from one track to the other would know anything like that. He had considered breaking into the D&RG offices to find bills of lading or shipping orders. Pauline's idea would pay off quicker—and not cause any ripples that might bring the law down on them.

"I met him once. The crew on General Palmer's train introduced me." Pauline hurried off, vanishing into the maze of trains with their heavy cars, leaving Slocum with the horses. He shifted nervously, not sure why he was so edgy. He jumped a foot when Pauline returned, grinning from ear to ear.

"I found it, John! I found out what happened to the car. It's being repaired."

Slocum's heart sank. "Repaired? They'll have found the gold."

"Maybe not. It was just taken off duty after a round-trip to Trinidad. Let's find out for sure."

Slocum led their horses through the tracks and cars to a large barnlike building. The doors were half-open, and inside he saw a freight car. His heart raced faster when he saw the number on the side.

3123.

"This is it," he said, double-checking to be certain it was a D&RG car. "Looks as if they were working on the wheels." He bent down and saw where iron rods had been rewelded on the underside of the car. The upper portion hadn't been touched as far as he could see. Straining, he got the heavy door pushed aside and jumped into the empty freight car.

"Where is the compartment?" asked Pauline, looking around the gloomy interior. Slocum lit a lucifer and let it sputter for a moment. He didn't have any idea where a secret compartment might be, but it wouldn't be on either side. That left the front or rear of the car, since Matt Burnside would have been too weak to lift a hundred pounds of gold to a rooftop compartment.

"On that point your brother's telegram wasn't too specific," Slocum said, dropping the lucifer when it burned his fingers. He went to the front of the car and tapped the panels. The sound was curiously hollow when it should have been solid. "This must be it."

Slocum worked for a few minutes, until he found the simple releases at the top and bottom of a panel. A quick twist of the screws caused the panel to drop off.

"Look at that," he said. In the six-inch-deep compartment lay the gold and stacks of greenbacks Matt Burnside had taken from the canvas bags and stuffed inside. "We're rich."

Just as the words left his lips, Slocum heard a six-shooter cock behind him.

"Don't," came the cold command. "I been wonderin' if you would find the gold. That looks mighty fine to me."

Slocum turned slowly and said, "You've never been too far away, have you, Warren?"

Phil Warren laughed harshly. "Not too far, Slocum. I made a bad mistake thinking you'd already got the last telegram from that kid up in Manitou—"

"You killed Andrew?" Pauline was shocked.

"And the girl with him. Couldn't have witnesses," Warren said, carefully getting into the freight car. He kept his six-shooter trained squarely on Slocum, knowing where the real danger would come from if anything went wrong for him. "And I saved your bacon out in the woods when that fat fool tried to gun you down. Couldn't have you dyin' on me before you found the gold."

"I was the only one with three of the four telegrams," Slocum said. "What happened to Durham?" Slocum judged his chances and saw they were poor. Phil Warren was a killer through and through. The only question in Slocum's mind was why Warren hadn't gunned him down before now.

"That deputy what got a wild hair up his ass caught Slick Bob," Warren said. "He was shot and killed, tryin' to escape, they said. I figure the deputy just upped and murdered him. Who knows?"

"You took the spare horse outside the hotel, up in Ruxton Park, didn't you?" Slocum wanted to keep Warren talking, but the coldness growing in the outlaw's eyes told Slocum he didn't have a snowball's chance in hell of doing that much longer.

"Why don't you stop jawin' and start movin' that gold? Bring it on over here by the door. I got me a horse all rigged out to carry it. You can load it for me. Then you can die."

"You're going to kill us?" Pauline's voice was small and frightened.

"Maybe not you," Warren said, leering at her. "If you got a hankerin' for a real man, we can get along just fine," he said. He took a quick step back and pointed the gun at Slocum's face. "Don't go gettin' any funny ideas about jumpin' me, Slocum. You're quick, but you're not that quick."

Slocum began pulling the gold from its hiding spot. He walked slowly, his mind racing. A hot breeze blew in the door from across the cindered rail yards. He hoped to see a railroad detective making his rounds, but no one was in sight. Some other way of distracting Warren would have to come up. Warren watched Slocum like a hawk as he secured the gold in the pack on the horse's back.

"The greenbacks now, Slocum. Don't leave a one behind. You help him, little lady." Warren motioned with his gun, and Slocum knew Phil Warren had no intention of taking Pauline with him. There would be two bodies in the car after the gold weighed down the packhorse.

"It's so hard to carry," Pauline protested, gathering an armload of paper money. "I'm not sure I can hold it all."

Slocum's hand was already going for his Colt Navy when Pauline stepped into the doorway. The hot wind caught her armload of greenbacks and sent them fluttering throughout the freight car. For a moment, the flying paper money obscured Warren's line of fire and caused him to instinctively reach up to brush away the cloud of bills.

Two shots rang out, Slocum's and Warren's.

For a moment both men froze. Then Warren sank slowly, as if someone had removed the bones from his legs.

"John, are you all right?" Pauline rushed to him and threw her arms around his neck. "I was so afraid. I didn't know if you'd be able to do anything when the wind caught the money."

"He's dead, but somebody might have heard the gunshots." Slocum gently pushed her back, knelt, and stuffed a handful of the fluttering bills into his shirt, then realized that getting greedy would put him behind bars. There wasn't enough time to collect all the greenbacks before the railroad detectives came to investigate.

"The horse is loaded with the gold. Let's ride." He jumped out of the car, leaving Warren in a pile of greenbacks. Scrip was well-nigh worthless, most folks discounted it. Why bother with it when he had a hundred pounds of real money, of bullion?

He helped Pauline down and handed her the reins of her horse.

"Where do we go, John?" she asked.

"Anywhere we want," Slocum told her, swinging into the saddle. It felt good being rich and with Pauline Yoakum. "Anywhere at all."

If you enjoyed this book, subscribe now and get...

TWO FREE

A $7.00 VALUE—

If you would like to read more of the very best, most exciting, adventurous, action-packed Westerns being published today, you'll want to subscribe to True Value's Western Home Subscription Service.

Each month the editors of True Value will select the 6 very best Westerns from America's leading publishers for special readers like you. You'll be able to preview these new titles as soon as they are published, *FREE* for ten days with no obligation!

TWO FREE BOOKS

When you subscribe, we'll send you your first month's shipment of the newest and best 6 Westerns for you to preview. With your first shipment, two of these books will be yours as our introductory gift to you absolutely *FREE* (a $7.00 value), regardless of what you decide to do. If

you like them, as much as we think you will, keep all six books but pay for just 4 at the low subscriber rate of just $2.75 each. If you decide to return them, keep 2 of the titles as our gift. No obligation.

Special Subscriber Savings

When you become a True Value subscriber you'll save money several ways. First, all regular monthly selections will be billed at the low subscriber price of just $2.75 each. That's at least a savings of $4.50 each month below the publishers price. Second, there is never any shipping, handling or other hidden charges—*Free home delivery*. What's more there is no minimum number of books you must buy, you may return any selection for full credit and you can cancel your subscription at any time. A TRUE VALUE!

A special offer for people who enjoy reading the best Westerns published today.

WESTERNS!

NO OBLIGATION

Mail the coupon below

To start your subscription and receive 2 FREE WESTERNS, fill out the coupon below and mail it today. We'll send your first shipment which includes 2 FREE BOOKS as soon as we receive it.

Mail To: **True Value Home Subscription Services, Inc. P.O. Box 5235**
120 Brighton Road, Clifton, New Jersey 07015-5235

YES! I want to start reviewing the very best Westerns being published today. Send me my first shipment of 6 Westerns for me to preview FREE for 10 days. If I decide to keep them, I'll pay for just 4 of the books at the low subscriber price of $2.75 each; a total $11.00 (a $21.00 value). Then each month I'll receive the 6 newest and best Westerns to preview Free for 10 days. If I'm not satisfied I may return them within 10 days and owe nothing. Otherwise I'll be billed at the special low subscriber rate of $2.75 each; a total of $16.50 (at least a $21.00 value) and save $4.50 off the publishers price. There are never any shipping, handling or other hidden charges. I understand I am under no obligation to purchase any number of books and I can cancel my subscription at any time, no questions asked. In any case the 2 FREE books are mine to keep.

Name _____

Street Address _____ Apt. No. _____

City _____ State _____ Zip Code _____

Telephone _____

Signature _____
(if under 18 parent or guardian must sign)   14294-9

Terms and prices subject to change. Orders subject
to acceptance by True Value Home Subscription
Services, Inc.